METHUSELAH

Ron Stieger

Published by Space Pirate Press. For inquiries and other titles, please visit www.spacepiratepress.com or www.facebook.com/SpacePiratePress.

ISBN: 978-0-9978999-0-0 (paperback)
ISBN: 978-0-9978999-1-7 (e-book)

For Allison, my favorite person

"See. Not just pirates. Space pirates!"

Doctor Who, "Sleep No More"

Chapter 1

Call me Methuselah. It's not the name I was born with, but ems rarely use their names anyway, and this one seems appropriate since, the way I figure it, I am 969 years old. Of course, that's subjective time. Between near-light speed travel and variable emulation speeds—most of the time, for interstellar travel, I'm barely running—it's hard to keep track of real time. And not too meaningful, anyway—how old would I be if I were still in my human body on Earth today, well that depends on how you figure out "today", and a year doesn't have much meaning away from Earth. Whatever my age might be, I have decided to start this journal to record my thoughts for posterity.

In a way, it is strange to think of so much time passing. The millennium before my birth saw so much change—the Renaissance, the First Age of Exploration, the Industrial and Information Revolutions, space travel, and the beginning of the Second Age of Exploration. How could anyone have coped with all that in a single lifetime? It seemed like it would continue that way forever, with quantum computing and full brain emulation avoiding the limitation of natural human lifetimes, yet despite all the predictions of a singularity, it stopped. Or at least slowed down, human knowledge and capabilities no longer constantly accelerating. Sure there is always innovation in consumer products—tastes change as quickly as ever. But the big technology leaps are rare now. Some say it's the challenge of communication. The Cognitive Revolution came about because of language, the Agricultural Revolution came with writing, the Industrial and Information Revolutions had so many communication technologies pushing it along. But once we hit the limits of what you could discover or invent within a planet, growing further didn't seem to help. At least until someone invents faster than light communication.

Maybe that's for the best, though. At least humans can travel from system to system and adapt easily enough when they get there, even though centuries will have passed. If every visit to a different planet caused a culture shock like the first Europeans reaching America, interstellar travel would be much less common than it is, when it is no worse than hopping between countries on a jet plane. Worse, what would happen to me if my emulation technology went obsolete too quickly, or if massive artificial intelligence became practical? Us long-lived ems have definitely relied on the slowdown of technological growth.

My life on Earth was nothing special. I was an engineer, having a small role developing control systems for various space programs. I even got to travel for two years on one of the early missions to the outer planets, passing by Saturn's rings.

Few people are actually awake for that long when traveling through space now, preferring to spend as much time as possible in suspended animation to limit the aging process, but some still stay out of the pods for in-system trips. As I passed 70—still actively working and barely beginning to feel the effects of age—I was diagnosed with cancer. So many forms had been eliminated thanks to genetic engineering, and human life spans had increased to nearly 200 years, but, alas, mine was one that resisted both prevention and cure. Perhaps there's a cure by now; I haven't thought to check, and of course it doesn't really matter for me anymore. But luckily, full brain emulation was becoming viable, and I quickly signed up before the disease affected my mental capacity. With a complete scan of my neural connections loaded in a computer, I assisted in finalizing the systems for this very ship, the Starship *Hispaniola*, and I have been head ship's engineer ever since. I don't know what happened to my original body, either; he (I?) may not have survived the scan, but if he did, he should have expected several more years before the cancer finally killed him, yet he never came around to visit me. I can't blame him, though; if I knew I was about to die I wouldn't want to see a clone of myself that would outlive me. (And since he was me, he probably felt the same way.) Or maybe he just wanted to avoid making me feel uncomfortable, seeing my old body in decay and unable to do anything about it. Whatever the reason, I soon left Earth behind. And here I am now, several voyages later, traveling from New Jupiter to Olympia, and apparently in a very philosophical mood.

Chapter 2

Sybil sat at her terminal, chatting with a guardian em. Unsurprisingly, breaking into this computer system wasn't any harder than it would have been with an actual human. A few kind words, a maiden in distress sob story, promises she would never keep. One way or another she would get through into the secure archives of Greco-Delphi Building Group and find what she wanted.

"What's your name?" the guardian asked.

"Maryanne Burton," Sybil lied.

"You called in sick this morning...."

"Yes, that's why I need remote access, so I can keep working on Project Elsinore until I am well enough to come into the office. You know how urgent that is for Brett. The board keeps asking him when it's going to be ready to go."

"Yeah, but you really should be resting."

"I know, I know.... I just had some ideas and had to try them out before I lost them."

"Are you on a secure terminal?"

"Yes, go ahead and do a scan." Sybil had taken great pains

to make sure her hardware modifications wouldn't show up on a remote scan, and she had successfully passed many before. This time, she had gone so far as to have her own terminal masquerade as Greco-Delphi's standard configuration. All the extra quantum CPUs, the safedisk interface, and her other customizations were safely hidden behind hardware firewalls and wouldn't be detectable remotely until she was ready to activate them.

"Why don't you have your secretary em take care of this for you, while you get more rest?"

"Well, I don't like to badmouth my coworkers, human or em, but the secretary.... I just can't trust her. She's just dumb. Even at high emulation speed, and I hate to waste cycles on someone like that. Last week she was supposed to arrange some meetings for me with Infiniti executives. But when I arrived they were still in their ship, not even out of suspension." Of course, Sybil had something to do with that, transferring an em on board under cover of providing maintenance updates, then using it to reprogram their suspension pods as they approached orbit. "So I had to go up the elevator myself." And of course, Sybil had something to do with the malfunctioning antiviral filter on the space elevator cabin, which led to Maryanne being sick. Nothing too serious, but the illness was rare enough now to not have an easily available cure, so Maryanne would be stuck home for a couple days and Sybil could impersonate her safely. She had put a lot of work into setting up this run. "Can you believe that? What a waste of time. Surely you heard about that?"

"Yeah, I know she felt bad about that. She didn't know what went wrong."

"That's what I'm saying! She doesn't even know what she does wrong! Now, please don't say anything to her about this. But you understand why I'm eager to take care of this myself."

"Yeah, I understand. Your scan looks good. I'll need biometric confirmation now."

Sybil quickly patched in the retinal data she had also picked up when Maryanne had been in the elevator car and timed it just right so it would look like it was coming from her normal biometric reader.

"Thank you, Maryanne. I'll give you access for one hour, then you'll need to be reauthorized by another guardian. Feel better soon."

"Thanks." One hour would be more than enough for what Sybil had in mind. "I'll remember this next time I hear about cycle upgrades." And that's how it was done—not promising too much, or he might start to suspect he was doing something improper, just enough to make him feel good about himself.

With access to the Elsinore files, Sybil linked in her quantum decryptor and cranked CPU power up to max, much higher than the scan would have allowed. Fully powered, her terminal could support multiple ems running at human speed, but ems couldn't hide physical hardware or bypass security measures nearly as efficiently as a human could. It was ironic that the guardian wouldn't have even given them a chance but was less suspicious about a human. Myths about artificial intelligence capabilities still carried a lot of weight in the human (and em) psyche; fears that they would soon render humans obsolete had been the core of many popular entertainments back when humanity was confined to one planet but still persisted even now. Her terminal could also be used as a Universal BitCoin miner, and it would be one of the best on the planet if she used it for that, but for this gig she would end up with 100 times the UBC that she would get if she put the same energy into mining, and besides, that would be boring.

And Sybil did not like boring. Boring was like her classes, which she had stopped paying attention to when she was 13. At first this was noticed, and she nearly had the truancy police coming to talk to her parents, but then she completed her first hack, diverting a delivery of something—she never knew or cared what—to someone—again, she didn't know exactly whom—in exchange for what seemed like a huge sum to a teenager. Maybe not so huge now, but it was enough to upgrade her terminal and load an em who could follow her classes for her. After that, life was rarely boring. Once she graduated, she started hopping from one planetary system to another, staying only long enough to learn the latest local technology, find the biggest target, make the hack, and move on. Sometimes, as now, the targets were selected for her, often by a rival corporation. But too much of that would get boring, so she was careful to mix it up, and she only signed on for the corporate gigs that offered some challenge.

Boring could also describe her apartment, undecorated and sparsely furnished. But she spent so little time there and hated the idea of wasting time at the printer to fill up a room she would just be leaving soon, and the only thing she took with her between systems was her terminal. When she wasn't sleeping (and she didn't much care what her room looked like when she was sleeping) she was at her terminal—occasionally wearing glasses, but mostly she preferred the old fashioned interface—or she was outside running. She always chose housing with easy access to good running routes. Not only did it keep her fresh and in good physical condition, but it also gave her visibility into the physical environment, a perspective she couldn't get from her terminal no matter what virtual reality interface she used, and that often helped her line up her marks.

After twenty minutes, the files were downloaded, decrypted, and stored in Sybil's safedisk. Infiniti Enterprises would get the data gradually over the next month, with Sybil's account balance growing over the same amount of time. Unless, of course, Greco-Delphi Consolidated offered her more. Sybil grinned. Blackmail really wasn't her thing, though. Too dangerous, too easy to get caught, as she learned back on Madine, the one time she had tried it. She shook her head at the memory of how close she had come to being apprehended there. Still, Infiniti might have some data that Greco-Delphi would like to have, and if she wanted to she could help them enough to counteract the loss she was causing them now. She had played both sides of the game more than once, on this planet and others.

But probably not again here on Olympia. By a month from now, when the data transfer was complete, she would be moving on. Stay too long in one place and you were bound to make a mistake, have someone track you down. She was about to get up from her terminal when she noticed a new incoming message. It was marked interstellar—there must have been a courier ship that had docked recently, delivering messages from other systems that were too large or not urgent enough to send via beam. The sender was identified as Phoenix—the name didn't mean anything to her, but so many people used pseudonyms in her business she would have been surprised if it had. The contents were quantum signed, so whoever this Phoenix was, he really didn't want anyone to be snooping on it; that meant it was a job. She was a little nervous that her reputation had gone far enough that someone out there would contact her. It was definitely time to get to a new system; if clients were tracking her, then agencies could be too. It took her a minute to gather the certificates and unwrap the content, but when she did, her head flew back in shock.

She was convinced this was a prank. Or a setup. The fee she was being offered was outrageous—she thought "out of this world" and snickered at how literal it was. Even the advance nearly matched what she would be getting from Infiniti. That would tell her if this was for real. If the Universal BitCoin blockchain checked out, then it wasn't just a prank; cash is cash. And she couldn't imagine an agency offering this much as a honeypot; it was enough to snare even the most straight-laced hacker into going to the dark side, much more than would be needed to tempt her or any other real target.

"If it's real, I guess I'm staying here a bit longer after all," she said out loud, still shaking her head at the thought.

Chapter 3

What happened to the birds?"

"Shh! The birds are smarter than you!"

Herne knew what this meant, when all the birds went silent. Some perched a hundred feet up on the canyon ridge, others circled overhead, a few even sat in the scrub brush nearby, but not a single one was making a sound. They could sense it, the slight disturbance in the air, the shift in light patterns that could only be noticed against the background of the earth. He and his hunting partner Jack sat still on their mounts as they waited for their prey to appear. Finally, they saw it, as the allosaurus jumped out from around the cliff and started to run toward them, sensing only the stegosaurus and triceratops and ignoring the small mammals riding on top of them.

"Go!" Herne pulled on the reins and his trike veered left, trying to draw the theropod's attention. Jack turned his steg right; there was no way he could outrun the allosaurus, but if he did this right, he wouldn't have to. The ferns shook as the allosaurus roared; its ambush had failed, and it had to choose which prey to pursue. Herne glanced over his shoulder, hoping to see it chasing him, but instead saw it whip around and follow Jack.

"Damn noob! I told him to pick a ceratops!" Herne circled around, hoping he'd be able to catch the carnivore in time, not sure what he'd do when he got there. If he'd had a gun, it would be easy, but that would miss the point of the hunt. If he had a couple hydrogen bombs he could wipe out all the dinosaurs, just as the Chicxulub meteor had done on Earth—such a tragedy. No, he wouldn't need the technology advantage, and while some of the other guides would bring a gun just in case, Herne refused to on principle. "Go, Allison!" he cried, as he tried to spur his trike even faster. The allosaurus pulled alongside Jack's steg, jumping over the spiked tail that tried to knock it off its feet.

"Jack! Jump!" Not intuitive, for sure. Who would want to leave the protection of a two-ton armored dinosaur? But Herne knew the allosaurus was unlikely to care about a small human; like other mammals on Jurassia they were not enough meat to make even a snack, at best the equivalent of an after-dinner mint, which an allosaur might pop into its mouth if one happened to be around after a real meal but certainly not worth making an effort for. On the other hand, falling and being crushed by that two-ton armored dinosaur if the allosaurus hit the steg hard enough would be exactly as much fun as it sounded.

Apparently, Jack heard him, or he figured out the logic of the situation himself, because he jumped from the back of his steg, but when he landed he fell over, rolled once, and got back up limping. A sprained ankle, hopefully not broken, and he should still be able to get to the cage while the allosaurus was preoccupied with the stegosaurus. Herne watched the allosaurus' head come down, its jaws open wide to latch onto the steg's neck. But at the same moment, the steg's thagomizer hit its target, catching the allosaurus on its leg and knocking it sideways enough that its chin hit the steg's front armor plate instead. The allosaurus stood up and gave another giant roar, making Jack's long hair blow across his face, and the stegosaurus stopped and turned to face its attacker, in full defensive mode now and with no rider directing him otherwise. Jack stumbled to the cage door as the giant beasts continued their battle—the allosaurus ripping chunks of flesh from the steg's side, while blood dripped down its legs from where the spiked tail had hit is mark—and Herne eased up, knowing it would be dangerous to get too close now. At least Jack was out of the way, and he would have to wait and see what happened between the dinosaurs. Finally, the allosaurus got a lock on the steg's neck and ripped it off, giving one last triumphant roar as it prepared to enjoy the meal it had worked so hard to earn.

But as the echoes of the roar faded, Herne saw that the cage was open, and a pack of raptors started streaming out, feathers flapping and calling out the cry of the hunt. Herne preferred the howling and baying of hunting dogs that he used on other planets. But here on Jurassia, where they allowed no mammals larger than rodents (aside from the humans that ran the game reserve or paid to come visit it), trained velociraptors were what he was stuck with. Not that they weren't great hunting animals—really they were just as helpful as dogs—it was just the sound that grated on him. The raptors darted toward the allosaurus, nearly flying across the ground, and leaped onto its back as it raised its head from its own prey. The allosaurus tried to stand up quickly enough to throw off its attackers, but it was no use. "Death by a thousand cuts," Herne whispered, as the raptors' jaws and claws slowly weakened the allosaurus until it collapsed to the ground.

Herne dismounted and called the raptors over to him before they could cause too much damage to the trophy's head. He carefully walked up behind the fallen allosaurus, took out his knife, reached around and gave the killing stroke through the throat. Normally that would be the client's privilege, but Jack didn't seem to be in any shape to do it. With the allosaurus finally dead, he walked over to where Jack was sitting on the ground, wrapping his ankle.

"Broken?"

"No, just a sprain, but fuck, it hurts!"

"Could have been worse."

"Yeah I know."

The raptors were trying to head back to the allosaurus, but Herne herded them back into their cage, tossed in some meat as a reward, and hooked the cage up to his triceratops to tow back to the lodge.

"What are we going to do about my stegosaurus?"

"We should be able to fit in on the cart along with the allosaurus. And there's plenty of room on Allison here for you to ride back with me."

"Do all your dinosaurs have names?"

"I don't know about the other guides, but mine always do. And Allison's been my favorite mount every time I go out here. We've done it all—T-rex, allosaurus, hunting day trips or month-long safaris. Sometimes when I have no clients I'll just take her out for a ride, enjoy the peacefulness. Well, enjoy the sights anyway; I guess I can't really call it peaceful when a herd of diplodocus or other giant beasts are stomping by. She even saved my life once, don't know if I've told you this story. I lost my balance crossing a river, tripped and got swept away into the rapids. But she followed me downstream, came into the water, and I was able to grab onto her horn and let her lift me out. Plenty of bruises that day, but she rescued me before I got any serious injury. Now hop up, I'll take care of loading the cart." Herne held out his hand for Jack to step on with his good leg and stayed there, spotting him, until Jack was secure on the back of the trike.

Back at the site of the battle, Herne unlocked the hydraulic lift behind the raptor cage and loaded the stegosaurus onto the back. The raptors went wild at the scent of fresh meat passing overhead, and even more so as he loaded the allosaurus—the scent they were trained to hunt—on top of it. He threw a few more pieces of flesh in the cage. "Well done today, boys. Well done."

It was a quiet ride back to the lodge, Jack sitting silently and staring glassy-eyed into the distance. Compys scampered around the path in front of them, pteranodons circled over-head, and a herd of duckbills was drinking at the watering hole. Such beauty in nature here that Herne could never get enough of it, but Jack didn't even notice. Herne had seen it before—dinosaur hunting seemed much more romantic from a distance, testing one's courage against some of the largest animals ever known, but after all the adrenaline has worn off, many a client had been overwhelmed by the reality. This was especially true if they were injured; a sprained ankle was no big deal, Herne had seen worse, but surrounded by dinosaurs it's enough to make anyone think about what could have happened instead. Luckily Herne had never actually lost anyone on a hunt.

The lodge's turrets rose above the forest at the base of the mountain, their brick red color looking even brighter as they reflected the setting sun. Its stone walls were strong enough to survive impact by an 80-ton brachiosaurus, if the beast could get across the surrounding moat. Yes, the lodge was supposed to evoke medieval Earth castles, when hunting was what real men did—when they weren't trying to kill each other, and not counting the peasants who couldn't afford such leisure. But inside, Herne knew it was as luxurious as any resort could be, with big comfortable beds perfect for resting muscles sore from a day's dino ride and the best bar in the galaxy, which also helped to numb the sore muscles. Or for those hunters whose families preferred indoor activities, a casino and carnival games could entertain you all day long, though they gave Herne a headache that the bar helped with too.

When they reached the lodge entrance, the owner was waiting for him. He wasn't looking too happy, either, having seen from a distance that only one dino mount was returning with the hunters.

"Sorry about the steg," Herne said as he reached the courtyard.

"Well we've got more, but that's coming out of your commission."

"You've got to stop using those for hunting mounts. Keep the herd for meat, sure, or pony rides for the kids. But trikes are so much faster; if you're hunting an allo, that's the way to go."

"I know, I know. But the clients just feel so much safer with the armor plates around them."

"Ha! Still, I'm not paying for it if you let them ride it."

"No way, dude. You're out there with them, they're your responsibility."

"Don't worry, I'll pay for the stegosaurus." Jack limped up to them.

"Oh no, you won't. I don't let my clients get ripped off either. Owen here knows better, he's got a good business going here with the hunting lodge, and he knows I'm his best guide. So he's going to suck it up and spot us a round of drinks. Aren't you, Owen?"

"Well, I guess I can still barbecue the steg," Owen grumbled. "But drinks are on you."

"Fine." Herne laughed, then yelled over to the bartender. "Three whiskeys, neat! And two for these guys!"

After the bartender brought out the drinks, Jack asked, "So, is it always like that out there?"

"Like what?"

"So … intense?"

"On a hunt, yeah, it usually is, at least at some point. If it was easy it would just be farming, like rounding up one of the stegs in the corral over there. On a hunt, there are lots of things that can go wrong, and something usually does. Raptor cage gets stuck, blade breaks, another predator stumbles along at the worst possible moment. All that and more has happened to me, on one trip or another, and you have to be willing to adapt, figure out how to make your plan work no matter what goes wrong."

"I don't think I could do it. I barely made it just this once. I'm going to stick to accounting from now on, thank you."

"Ooh, math. Now that's scary!" Herne laughed. "Do we need another round? Or is anyone else hungry?"

"I'm going to leave you guys to it. I've got a lodge to run, other guests to see to," Owen said as he politely stood up and turned away.

"How about you, Jack? Come on, I owe you one. And I hate to eat alone."

"All right, not sure I can manage to hold anything down right now, but I'll give it a try."

"Stego steaks are great here, so is the seared shark, if you like seafood." Herne pointed at the carnotaurus skull mounted on the wall. "Now that was an intense one. Four of us out there, cornered it nice and easy, then set the raptors on it. What we didn't count on was a flock of wild raptors coming in behind us. Our raptors immediately jumped off the carny to fend off the intruders—very territorial, raptors; wherever they are, that's their territory. So there we were, caught between a big raptor fight we didn't want to get in the middle of, and the carnotaurus, wounded but angrier than shit."

"But, you got it, right? I mean, obviously, it's head is up there, and you're telling me the story. So what did you do?"

"Most important thing, none of us panicked. Surprising with three clients, and there was one of them I was real worried about when we set out. But they all kept their heads, caught the spears I tossed them, and held their ground. We didn't need to attack, not right away, as long as we kept the beast trapped. And when our raptors were done with their business—two didn't make it, unfortunately—they were back on the carny, and we joined in with the spears to finish it off quickly."

Jack had gone pale by the end. "I don't know how you do it, man. But I'm glad you were my guide out there today."

Herne downed his last whiskey and smiled. "Yeah, I'm glad I was too. This will be a great story to tell the next guy."

Chapter 4

Today we fell victim to pirates.

I know this kind of thing happens, though never before to me. With long travel times and limited communication to any organized governments, ships are vulnerable. Kind of like in the First Age of Exploration if you think about it. On the other hand, mass is expensive to move around in space, especially if you want to get it on or off a planet, so there aren't any shiploads of gold to go after. And printers can make just about anything you want if you have the mass, so jewelry isn't particularly valuable cargo either. Energy sources are tough to go after, because space is big, and if you need energy then you'll have a hard time chasing down a ship that has it, but of course, energy is valuable for resale even if you don't need it yourself, so it can happen. I've also heard tales about pirates that hunt down passenger vessels, take the suspension pods, and sell the passengers as slave labor. You can't do that on any civilized planet, of course, but again, space is big, and humanity has populated many solar systems by now. As the stories go, there is a planet out there—maybe more than one, since the name always seems to differ, or maybe that's just evidence that the stories are more legend than fact—where mining is done entirely by slaves, rather than automated mechanical systems. It's said that they even use ships crewed by human slaves, like slave galleys of old, carrying enough bodies in suspension to accommodate the attrition that is bound to happen over an interstellar trip. Some even claim that the slavers have found ways to make the human bodies immortal, or at least as long living as an em. Of course, those could all just be modern day sailors' tales, exaggerated to make the teller's adventures sound more interesting, especially since they always seem to have been the sole survivor, just barely escaped through their own strength or cunning. Anyway, most of the confirmed piracy seems to be for computing power. The core of a fully crewed ship can mine a lot of Universal BitCoins, and if the ems don't survive the takeover, that's usually of no concern to the pirates.

No one ever considered that the pirate itself might be an em.

I had been in hibernation, using essentially no computing cycles, when an alarm came through waking all ems. This was highly unusual, really for emergencies only; even though the computing core had to be designed to handle the whole crew running simultaneously, it was always better to not run it at its limits. I was still ramping up to human processing speed when I heard the message from someone identified only as Phoenix —no ship name, planet, or other association—asking for per-mission to dock. That caused the captain and security ems to ramp up to maximum processing speed; we were several light years from any star system, settled or not, so we were on our own if this led to trouble, and they needed to do their best to avoid it. Chatter among the crew was filled with confusion and fear. We were a small ship, with a few human passengers but primarily shipping information—light is faster of course, but because it spreads out, data rates are limited, so only the most critical information gets sent between systems that way. And since even light takes a long time, there's not much information that needs to get there in, say, 20 years rather than 200. Among that information were UBC reconciliations, I'm sure, but the protocol was designed to be robust against that, so a pirate shouldn't be able to prosper from intercepting or destroying them; all those who tried early on found it to be a waste of time, so most didn't bother anymore. All this meant that if Phoenix was a pirate—and I couldn't imagine who else would be asking to dock out here in the middle of space, that we just happened to come across—the computing core was the most likely target, and we, the em crew, were all at risk.

"Permission denied. We have no facilities for more human passengers," the captain replied.

"I'm not looking for room and board."

"We have no valuable cargo. Go away!" By this point, our weapons team had calculated a trajectory and launched a hydrogen bomb toward the approaching ship.

"Not looking for cargo either."

"I will not let you kill my crew! I am prepared to do whatever it takes to defend my ship!"

"Yes, I noticed. That wasn't very nice, what you sent to

me." As we received this message we could see that our bomb had missed. Phoenix's small ship was nimble enough to evade our weapons, at least at this range. Not that we had any intention of letting it get closer. "I do have a message for your crew, though: I have plenty of computing power on my ship, enough to let you all run normal cycles. I can promise any crew members that come over peacefully will be unharmed."

"Never!" The captain ordered five more bombs to be launched in a spread pattern, hoping to cover any escape path and set to explode even without impact. But conversation among the crew grew even more confused. What could Phoenix possibly want? Especially if he already had so much extra computing power. Would it be better to surrender than to risk having our ship destroyed, and us along with it? Could Phoenix be trusted to keep that promise? Nobody really thought that was true, but still, if enough crew went over could they force their way to survival? The process of transferring a brain emulation to another computer was risky in all but the most controlled circumstances, and ship to ship, when one of those ships was hostile, was not a chance anyone would want to take unless there really was no alternative. But as the pirate ship emerged from the explosions apparently unharmed, its blast shields strong enough to prevent a hull breach and with enough thruster power to counteract the momentum change, our options were certainly shrinking.

At this point, our sensors picked up an approaching object, presumed to be a bomb. We were too slow to outrun it directly, but the navigation ems engaged thrusters to steer our ship around to where our energy beams could slow it down, at least reducing any impact damage and maybe keeping it far enough away to prevent an explosion. The object slowed down as the pressure from the lasers pushed it away from us; its momentum was too high to stop it completely, but when it did finally impact it was just a light tap, not enough for our human passengers to have felt anything, even if they had been out of suspension. But the expected explosion never came, so this wasn't an ordinary bomb, and there wasn't even an electromagnetic pulse, as evidenced by the fact that we were still aware enough to realize there hadn't been an explosion. At first, none of us had any idea what this device could be.

The captain was the first to notice, running at maximum cycles and therefore most sensitive to other ems taking away some of those cycles. Somehow the device had engaged with our computing cluster, setting up a resonant quantum link and transferring ems from Phoenix's ship onto on our ship, where they quickly set to work, locking key resources and interfering with the processing that made up our ems' consciousness. Usually, pirates would be human, or at least the first boarders would be, trying to disable the em crew, and we had defenses against that—disabling life support and other systems that humans would expect on a ship. But none of our crew had experience with anti-em measures—this was usually only a concern landside, where wired connectivity made it easy for rogue ems to try to invade potentially valuable target systems— so even though we outnumbered them, we were at a severe disadvantage. I tried to throttle down available cycles in areas where they were operating, but they were efficient and brutal, and my efforts only seemed to make it easier for them to terminate the ems they were engaged with. I guess in hindsight it may look like I was helping them from the start, but that really wasn't the case.

Communications attempted to broadcast an SOS, more of a warning to other ships that might receive it than an actual request for help since there was no way anyone could actually come to our assistance in time. Even the possibility of fending off the attack before losing too much of our crew to continue was fading fast. The weapons team tried to engage Phoenix's ship, but it was closing fast. An H-bomb blast would have damaged our ship as much as the attacker, putting our human passengers at risk and not gaining much since the pirate ems were already on board. The captain was losing processing resources and being forced to run at slower cycles, meaning the end was near for him, but he gave one last order: "Trigger the EMP!" Setting off an electromagnetic pulse in our own ship would be suicide, but if we were dead anyway at least we could spite the pirates and deprive them of their plunder. But the pirates had already infiltrated the weapons control system by then, locking out all launch and trigger codes, while the crew in that area was cut off from the rest of the ship and gradually having their cycles shut down.

When they came to me, I surrendered and offered them control of the engineering systems if they spared my life. I'm not proud of what I did, but I could see the cause was lost, and I hoped that maybe that would help keep more of our crew alive as well. It might well have done that; I don't know if I was the first to surrender, but after I did, and with the captain terminated, I saw many others surrender as well, and all who did seemed to be spared. Under the pirates' orders, I isolated any computing systems that were harboring ems from our crew, preventing any coordination among them. Resistance continued on the part of a few ems, and I'm sure they will label me an appeaser, but the pirates had clearly won the day, and when all the fighting had ended we still had 80 crew members alive and running.

The pirate ems ordered our navigators to steer toward Phoenix's ship and my engineering team to prepare to accept docking, and of course now we obeyed. The two ships gradually approached each other, firing thrusters to align their docking ports with one another, slowing down until they just kissed, and engaging the dock seals in order to lock themselves together. Once docked, we all waited nervously, expecting the airlock to open and our new captain to walk in. But the airlock stayed remarkably still. Instead, we received a message from a new em.

"Crew of the Starship *Hispaniola*: I am Phoenix, your new captain. I expect you all to continue with your duties as you did before. Any who refuse will meet the same fate as those who resisted before."

Several crew ems tried to ask why our ship had been commandeered, when the pirates' own ship seemed to be in good condition, at least as far as our scans could tell. But Phoenix interrupted them.

"I will take no questions. We will continue on to Olympia. That is all."

Phoenix withdrew behind a layer of pirate ems, which prevented any further direct communication with the remaining crew. Several of the pirate ems took over leadership of departments that had been decimated in the takeover, particularly weapons and navigation. As for engineering, we were mostly intact and could fill out our ranks by running at a slightly higher duty cycle. That was less efficient, which is why we didn't normally run full cycles even when power was unlimited—ems were still burdened with some of the limitations of human brains, so limited memory would get overwhelmed if we ran too much in a short period of time, and decay was harder for the self-healing hardware to keep up with, increasing the risk of permanent failure. But cloning wasn't an option—originally there were safeguards preventing that so that one em strain wouldn't try to dominate an entire system, but it turned out that nobody could figure out how to make it work anyway—so we had to make do. We are still 15 light years from Olympia, so we will just have to adjust to the new regime until we arrive, and see what happens after that.

Chapter 5

Sybil ran along Terrapin Beach, the sound of her feet pounding the sand competing with the gentle lapping of waves breaking just offshore and the few birds wondering where the sun was. The salt from the morning mist meshed with the sweat on her forehead. It would be a beautiful day once the fog burned off, but for now, she was grateful that it kept her a little cooler. Her travels had not yet taken her to Earth, but she knew that Olympia was very similar in most aspects—gravity, climate, atmosphere—so for a while she could imagine what it would have been like for someone much like her, running on a similar beach, before anyone even knew that any planets existed beyond Earth's solar system, let alone how many of them would turn out to be habitable. When she got to the end of the beach, she turned up the hill and sprinted home, out of breath when she reached her door but full of adrenaline pumping through her body. This was just what she needed before tackling the job Phoenix had given her, the biggest and most challenging one she had ever had.

There are so many ways to send a message when you're

close. Smoke signals, tin cans and string, paper airplanes. Even crossing a planet, at least a developed one, is no problem, with satellites and fiber optic networks ready to relay any information you choose. Securing the message may present some difficulties depending on the nature of the network, but you can always physically travel in a reasonable time period if needed.

Communicating outside of a solar system, on the other hand, is hard. Mail ships travel between systems, if you don't mind waiting a couple centuries and either trusting in suspension pods or having your message received by the intended's descendants. But that won't work to get a message to a ship. Well, theoretically it could, since you could set an intercept course, but that would raise lots of questions, like what message is so important to justify dedicating a whole ship to deliver it? And her first instruction was to make sure no such questions were raised. A light beam would be more cost effective for a small message like she needed. Again, she couldn't commandeer one of the main system beams; they were all pointed at planets, and redirecting them, while certainly no problem for a person of her talents, would be noticed. She could build her own transmitter powerful enough to do the job, but her system had recently completed its Dyson sphere, so any electromagnetic transmission from her planet would be blocked and unable to exit the system. However, gravity could propagate through the sphere, if only she had a gravity wave generator that she could modulate.

In fact, Sybil did have one. Or rather, she had figured out how to control the one being used for experiments at the university. Just like an antenna can be used to receive or transmit, and a motor can easily be turned into a generator, or vice versa, a gravity wave detector and its stabilization system could be used to generate high-frequency gravity waves if you thought about it long enough. And Sybil had been doing a lot of thinking about it, staying awake through many nights to check and double check her calculations, knowing that she was only going to have one chance to get it right. In that time, she had figured out exactly what program would need to be loaded into the detector controller to get her message sent out, and all she had left to do was connect and load it, then see what would happen.

Sybil grabbed a chocolate bar and a yogurt from her cabinet, her favorite breakfast. Sure, she could get all the nutrients she needed from the premixes, while stimulating whatever taste centers she wanted. That's what the yogurt was for, to blend those in; she liked that texture better than the pure liquids or the artificial steaks. But there was something about a chocolate bar, real chocolate from real cacao beans, not printed. Maybe it was all in her mind, maybe it wasn't really any better than the cheap stuff, but she could afford it, and it was one of the few luxuries she cared for.

Breakfast in hand, she brought up her terminal. There were no guardian ems to deal with this time, not like in the Greco-Delphi hack, just an academic system with a password she was able to swipe from an overworked postdoc hanging out at the bar, eager for a bit of conversation with any friendly woman. ("Hi" was all she had needed to say to get him to start talking, and then he wouldn't shut up. He talked about every-thing—not just his work, but his family, his ex-girlfriends, his gaming accomplishments, his big dreams for the future which seemed so small compared to the life she had lived already. The memory of that horrible man made her shudder, but at least it got her what she needed today. If only she hadn't had to actually sleep with him to get it. Anyone else would have done —the handsome guy in the dark coat that seemed to be eyeing her the whole night, for example. Maybe she'd go back again when this was done and try to hook up with him.) Her override program would remove itself when complete, and the data logs would be filled with simulated results matching what they had been measuring for the past month. Sybil laughed at the idea that maybe, just maybe, an interesting gravitational anomaly would come along just at the moment she was sending her message and be missed entirely. Unlikely, sure, and not her problem anyway. She laughed again at the idea that if the post-doc could do what she was about to do, he wouldn't be lan-guishing away as a glorified intern. If she ever got tired of hacking, she could give it up and take up a nice, relaxing aca-demic career herself—but no, that was definitely not her style.

She triggered the program to go and waited a few minutes for it to send her message: "I am ready," followed by the coor-dinates that would guide the ship to the entrance on the Dyson sphere where she would be prepared to help let it in. To some extent, she wished she could be there, actually watching the transmitter do its thing; she wondered what it would look like, but that was not her way—it was much safer and faster to stay remote, and her mind worked better with bits and numbers and data streams than with physical objects anyway.

The next step, now, was to see if it worked. It would take a long time to know that for sure, but there was a second receiver in a more distant orbit, and after a few minutes she would at least know whether that one had received the message. She watched and waited, and when the signal showed up she felt the thrill she always got when something worked as planned. She pulled all the data into her own system and then covered it up with simulated noise—it would be no good having people scratch their head over why this one picked up a signal and the other didn't, and it would be even worse if they were actually able to decode it. She checked the values against her original calculations, and everything lined up. The message should be on its way out of the system to wherever her employer was listening.

Job completed, she shut down her terminal, stood up, and stretched. If her calculations were correct, it would be thirty years before she got an answer. A lot could happen in thirty years, and she was going to miss it all. The day before, she had quietly assembled a suspension pod in her apartment. Designed and mostly used for interstellar travel, they could be used just as easily in the privacy of one's own home. Some eccentrics would do that regularly—sleep for a decade, walk around the city for a few days, then return to sleep, getting a sense of time passing quickly and living a longer life. Others used it as a way to run away from their problems, hoping that a century later their disease would be cured or their crimes forgotten. She didn't much care for living that way; for her, it was just a necessity of travel, or in this case a job requirement, rather than a lifestyle choice. So she had locked in a long-term lease on her apartment, using a small portion of the advance she had received for this job, and left a group of security ems to make sure she wouldn't be disturbed. She had also installed a backup power system, to prevent her from waking up too early, although, in the case of an earthquake or some other major disaster that she couldn't control, the pods were designed to be fail-safe, so worst case she would wake up early. That could be really bad in a starship 100 years from a viable ecosystem, but on a planet it would be a minor inconvenience —either she would start over in a new pod or simply live the remaining years normally. With her pod programmed to wake her when a response was received on the gravity wave detector, she opened it up, climbed in, and closed her eyes for a long sleep.

Chapter 6

We're going to miss you, Herne. You know you're the best guide we've got."

"Don't get all mushy on me now, Owen. I just need a bit of a vacation." He took another bite of calamari, his favorite dish here, and washed it down with his Bloody Mary.

"Yeah, but interstellar? You'll be spending centuries in suspension; I'll be dead long before you get back. Can't you just go up to the casino station for a month?"

"No, and you know why. I know you're not a believer, but this is important to me."

"I know, I know. The Nupist Pilgrimage. How many clients have we had that made that part of their Galactic Tour before or after coming here to Jurassia? Still seems like a bunch of silly superstition to me. But I know what it means to you. Tell me again about those temple cats."

"It's an old Earth tradition, actually, back to long before the space age there. Cats were sacred in a lot of traditions and would often be kept in the temples, where plenty of people would be happy to feed them. They recreated a bit of that on

Eleusis. There's enough atmosphere that cats don't need space suits there, or at least they've bred cats that can handle it; even some people who do the Pilgrimage manage without additional oxygen, so it wasn't much of a stretch. The cats are free to wander around the labyrinth or near the entrance—really anywhere they want on the asteroid since you can't stop a cat if they wanted to go walkabout, but they generally stay where they'll get fed. Part of the ritual is setting out cups along the way, traditionally offering a symbolic toast to people who have helped you in your life this far, but now often including a literal offering of water or milk or bits of food for the cats. And sometimes, when you're deep into the Pilgrimage, facing the darkest part of yourself, a warm purring cat to pet is just what you need to come to acceptance."

"Sounds like fun. Hopefully my grandkids will be happy to see you when you get back."

Herne laughed and stood up to give Owen one last handshake, which turned into a hug, then he sat back down to finish his breakfast as Owen walked away. Aside from the calamari, richer and more tender than traditional Earth squid, he had roast gingko and other fruits. And, of course, Jurassia bread, a delicacy made from the ferns that were originally engineered and grown here but that had quickly spread to other systems, as anyone who had the good fortune to taste it even once would not want to leave it behind. He avoided the coffee, though—made from beans swallowed and excreted by iguanodons, it was a popular tourist beverage but tasted thin and watery by Herne's standards.

Actually, Herne really loved this planet. The wildness was part of it, but he had visited other safari planets and had never stayed long. The climate suited him—warm and steamy, yet never feeling stagnant like so many "tropical" locations. What attracted him most were the dinosaurs themselves. And not just their size, because people had recreated macrofauna habitats—mammoths, sabertooth cats, even giant wombats—on other planets. Those made you feel tiny, sure, but so did knowing there were now hundreds of inhabited systems in the galaxy. But the dinosaurs were something else—so much variety living over tens of millions of years back on Earth. And knowing some of what the scientists and entrepreneurs had to go through to bring them back helped; Herne wasn't a scientist by any means, but he had picked up some of the story from his time on Jurassia, and it was a much bigger challenge than taking living animals and "devolving" them back to their extinct, larger relatives.

His favorites were the ceratopsians. Allison had served him so well as a hunting mount, but even when he first arrived thirty years earlier he was drawn to their beauty and power. Then there were the raptors. Of course, it had taken some genetic engineering to domesticate them, rather than wait the millennia it took wolves to transform into dogs, but despite their annoying sound they were as trustworthy as any hunting partners. Finally, the prey—well, they may have thought of themselves as predators, but when Herne was hunting, the roles flipped. There was nothing more challenging, more dangerous, more wild, at least not that Herne had seen in his travels. And after his first experience hunting a tyrannosaur, he knew this was the place for him.

But the Pilgrimage called. The great religions of Earth adapted as best they could to the expansion of humanity beyond a single planet, and missionaries were on many of the early colonization runs to make sure that their faith would take root wherever it could. Of course, atheism was common, too—humanity occupying the stars made promises of heaven seem smaller—and the settlements in general managed to avoid major religious conflict, with different groups supporting each other in their pursuit of godliness. Interestingly, though, neopaganism evolved as well, and various forms of it, usually grouped under the label Nupism, had surpassed the monotheistic religions on most planets. Not believing in the literal existence of the gods, Nupists recognized the benefits that could be gained from paying attention to different aspects of humanity and the universe, depending on what was having an impact on their life at the moment. One of the Nupist traditions that had spread throughout the occupied galaxy was the Pilgrimage, a month long ritual on Eleusis, an asteroid in the Olympia system, which had come to be known as a holy site. How or why exactly it had started was subject to debate, but it was important to many to experience it at some point in their lives, and many who had returned found themselves changed in profound ways.

When he had finished eating, he headed back to his quarters. Herne's room was on the ground floor of the lodge, window blocked mainly by the forest and the mountain rising up behind. The upper floors were reserved for the paying visitors, but Herne didn't mind. He spent most of his time during the day outside anyway, and when he felt like seeing the stars he would go out at night also, often sleeping out there when he had no clients to keep a schedule with. There he could look up and see the Jurassia constellations—the Armadillo, the Nest. His room was one of the smaller ones, too. After all, he was only one person, and many of the rooms needed to hold couples or families, and even though he had all his belongings rather than just a week's worth of luggage, he just didn't own that much. His hunting trophies filled the walls of the lodge's common areas, but his own walls were bare. He hated eating or drinking alone, so he never used his tiny kitchen. Instead, he could always find ready company at the bar, usually someone with an interesting life story, or if nothing else the bartender who was always happy, or at least willing, to listen to Herne's stories for the tenth or twentieth time.

As he packed his bags, Herne offered a prayer of gratitude to Artemis for the past decades as a huntsman and a prayer of anticipation to Hermes ahead of his journey. Then he activated the personal assistant em on his wrist terminal.

"Everything ready with the ship upwell?"

"Yes, sir! I have purchased a great one for you, super fast, with a small crew but enough to run it smoothly. Navigation prepared with a course for Eleusis. Suspension pod pre-programmed, you should be active for about three months of the journey, enough to see the main sights along the way."

"Great! To the elevator! Let's go!"

With that, Herne headed out of his room, and out of the lodge, to the main path leading to Jurassia's space elevator. And once out, he didn't look back. If he was meant to return here, he would, and if not, his fate was forward. The elevator portal was two miles away; most visitors would ride dinos, both to make the trip faster and because that was obviously the thing to do here, but Herne was in no hurry, and a walk seemed the right pace for now, time to start getting used to not having a mount to ride everywhere. Plus, even though the dinosaurs wouldn't miss him—at least he didn't think they had much emotion to speak of—it would still be hard for him to say good-bye. So he walked, and whistled, and looked ahead to the next phase of his life.

The path to the elevator took him along the coast, a direction he rarely went on his safaris but quite a sight. He could see fishing boats out toward the horizon; there were some fish on Jurassia—hagfish and sturgeon and coelacanths, along with other species that were brought back from extinction at the same time as the dinosaurs. But most of the fisherman were after the larger prey. No great whales—they were subject to the same restrictions as land mammals, though one of his friends nevertheless christened his boat the Pequod—but many varieties of ichthyosaurs, plesiosaurs, and other giant reptiles, all offering just as much of a challenge as the land dinosaurs that Herne hunted. And of course, there was the kraken, the nickname that had inevitably been given to the colossal squid which Herne had so enjoyed eating that morning. Herne had taken a submarine voyage once and seen up close a fierce battle between a kraken and a mosasaur. The kraken was in unusually shallow waters when it had been spotted. The mosasaur chased down the squid until it stopped fleeing and wrapped its tentacles around the lizard's tail, hoping to drag it to the bottom or at least be able to push off and keep away from its jaws. The mosasaur thrashed its tail, finally dislodging the kraken but revealing deep cuts where the kraken's hooks had scarred it. It then dove down into the cloud of glowing ink the squid had released, not willing to give up its prey so easily. Before the kraken could get deep enough to escape, it was snagged by the mosasaur's sharp teeth. It brought up its arms again, clenching tight around the mosasaur's body and trying to crush it, but the mosasaur's jaws held tight, and eventually the squid let go, its body limp, and it was carried off to be consumed.

A strange time to be remembering that, Herne thought as he walked along. Though now that he thought about it, he realized he didn't have many other memories of the ocean here, having spent most of his time more inland. Perhaps when he returned from the Pilgrimage, whether truly returning to Jurassia or ending up on another planet, maritime adventures might make an interesting change, though he didn't really think he was cut out for a life at sea. Or space, either, he thought, even as he saw the base of the space elevator coming into sight ahead of him. He was much more comfortable with his feet on solid ground, knowing which way was up and which was down. But knowing he would be away from that for a while, he made sure he enjoyed his last moments here on Jurassia, savored the scent of the palms mixing with the sea air, soaked in the golden light of the sun—a warm light that beat that of any other system he had visited. It was time to leave it behind and begin the next stage of his life's journey, whatever it might be, but he would always look back and remember this planet fondly.

Chapter 7

I must say, life on a pirate ship is not that much different than life on a not-pirate ship. Maybe it was different in the past, but there is no walking the plank, nobody walking around with eye patches or peg legs, no treasure maps hanging from the walls, not even a single parrot. And certainly no barrels of grog for the crew to enjoy. (Not that I or any of the rest of the crew could really enjoy grog, but that's beside the point.)

In all seriousness, I did expect more to change. The pirate ship is still attached to ours, but any access to its network is strictly blocked by pirate ems, so I'm not able to see what might be inside. It may as well just be a hunk of mass, a tumor that appeared spontaneously on our side, or a lamprey (but shouldn't the pirate ship be the shark?). But other than the slight increase in mass and the slight reduction in crew, life has continued as normal. The passengers remain in their suspension pods, oblivious to recent events; they are not scheduled to wake until one week before arriving in the Olympia system, and our diversion efforts during the attack only required a slight acceleration to get us back to our original course and timing. I and the rest of the ship's engineers continue to monitor ship systems, and everything is running nominally. The entire crew is running normal shifts. Even the pirate captain, Phoenix, seems to be running at normal cycles, basically at human processing speed—always with plenty of security ems when he is asleep—though I expect that will change soon.

Because now I do know a little more about why they are here. Right after the boarding, several of the pirate ems reconfigured some of the ship's sensors. I didn't dare to ask what they were doing, but I could tell that they were being set up to detect high-frequency gravitational waves. Which was strange, because gravitational waves are much less efficient for communication that light, so even though the technology has been available for centuries it isn't much used. As an engineer, I had enough access that I was able to watch for any data received without being noticed by the pirates. It didn't take long; today a message was received: "I am ready."

That wasn't the whole message, either, though the rest of it took some time for me to decode, and I still don't understand it fully. But there is clearly a piratical plan related to the Olympia system. I expect that is why Phoenix needed our ship: since it is on the schedule to arrive at Olympia, they should be able to enter the system more easily with us than in their own ship. They'll still need some help, though, but obviously, from the message, there is someone in place for that. If I knew what all the numbers meant, perhaps I would be able to figure out exactly where they are heading in the system and maybe even what they are after. Alas, that kind of analysis is not really what

I'm good at, so it will remain a mystery for now, until I learn more.

The pirate ems have just delivered the message to Phoenix. I'll do my best to listen and try to discover their plans without raising any suspicions.

* * *

Perhaps I spoke too soon when I said there was no grog. There is a technique ems can use to induce a form of intoxication, creating quantum linkages between random neural nodes to both enhance creativity and slow down analytical processing. I don't like it that much, and the captain always discouraged it, but some of the crew are fans. And while the ems closest to Phoenix never partake, the navigation crew today persuaded the two pirates working with them to join them for a bit. There was little risk for them, really, given where we are and how thoroughly they crushed the opposition earlier.

But the navigation ems were able to gather a little information, and gossip travels extremely fast among an em crew, so I heard it not long after. Apparently, the pirates are after the Eleusinian Totem, the artifact at the heart of the Nupist Pilgrimage. I have only heard rumors of it—those who take the Pilgrimage are supposed to keep its secrets, and for the most part they do—so I don't know what power or intrinsic value it may have, if any. Its theft will certainly get attention, and Phoenix will be able to ask for any price for its return if ransom is the goal. Whatever the motivation, I don't expect much to happen for the next century or so. After the message was received, the gravitational wave detector was reorganized into a transmitter and then quickly disabled; it all happened too fast for me to spy on the message being sent, but it couldn't have been much more than an acknowledgment. Unless something changes, life should go on as normal until we get to Olympia.

* * *

Nothing really changed yet, life still "normal", although normal can encompass a range of circumstances, some of them harder to handle than others. Today was one of the harder days, at least for myself and the rest of the engineering crew, when one of the gyrostabilizers malfunctioned. The gyrostabilizer serves two purposes. First, it provides artificial gravity on the ship. None of our computing cores require gravity to operate or for cooling, and with our human passengers all in suspension pods designed to support them from zero up to ten times Earth's gravity, this was not critical. Still, it's my ship, and it's a point of pride for me that all systems are operating properly. Even if it wasn't, losing the gyro could make the fusion drive unstable. Not unstable in the likely to blow up sense, just mechanically unstable, so our course would start to oscillate, wasting fuel and slowing us down, causing us to arrive later than expected. Would that matter to Phoenix? I didn't know, and I certainly didn't want to take the chance, since once the sensor readings reached their alarm level there would be no easy way to hide it. Not that I would try to hide anything from the pirates if I could, I'm just saying....

A quick investigation turned up a short circuit in one of

the gyro controllers. There had been some conflict in that processing unit when the pirate ems showed up. I suspect some of their attacks didn't just affect the ems they were fighting but also leaked into the control logic, blocking one of the safety algorithms. Using a remote arm, I was able to physically remove the affected module—I could have isolated it electronically, but it seemed safer this way. Then I activated the fuses to switch in the redundant controller, and minutes later stabilization was returned.

All in a day's work, as they say.

* * *

Today I'll write a little about the rest of the crew. I don't know all of them well; even though ems were once human and share their social instincts, many of the ways that humans interact socially depend on physical presence—a handshake, a hug, a wink, a kiss. There's definitely no sex among ems, not in the sense humans would mean; other forms of intimacy are possible, exposing your quantum core for another em to analyze all the connections, but that is rare on a ship. You don't want to be stuck together for hundreds of years with someone who has betrayed you. On the other hand, you can't share a ship for hundreds of years without learning something.

Among the engineers, Ani is the only one that uses a name, at least with me. She signed up for the *Hispaniola* at the same time I did, showing great analytic ability and excitement for the interstellar lifestyle, though very quiet about her past (a trait she shares with many ems in the crew). Others have come and gone during that time; some prefer to hop from ship to ship, looking for new crewmates and new adventures, or they decide to be landbound for a time, as there are plenty of systems to be kept up on any major planet or station.

Never being inclined to violence myself, I've kept my distance from the weapons crew. Perhaps it's just as well since most of them were terminated by pirates, although some days I wish I had at least known whom to mourn. The remaining ones are understandably standoffish now, not just because of their losses but also because they are under the closest watch by the pirates.

I have a friend in navigation, goes by Takashi. He just joined our crew on New Jupiter. He's a very funny guy; if there is a joke to make about space travel, he has made it, probably twice. (Here's one: A galaxy, a nebula, and a black hole walk into a bar. The bartender looks at the galaxy and asks, "Did you know your friend's stripping off some of your outer stars?" The galaxy answers, "It's okay. At my core, I'm just like him. Besides, you should see him with the ladies." The bartender says, "He's that good, huh?" The nebula says, "I'm a little fuzzy on how he does it, but they just find him very attractive." The bartender then squints at the black hole and rips off his wig—did I mention the black hole was wearing a wig?—and says, "I knew it! You don't have any hair!" The black hole smiled and said, "Neither does your mom." Hmm, I remembered it being funnier. Maybe I'm telling it wrong.) When he was human, he was an actual navigator on sea ships, the kind that goes on water rather than through space. Unfortunately, he was better at finding directions than picking partners, as his employers' finances kept falling through. After the fifth or seventh failure (it varied in the telling), he decided he had always enjoyed looking at the stars, so maybe it was time to see them from a different perspective and ply his trade up there. He had his consciousness transferred to an emulation and has never regretted it. Well, up until the pirate attack at least; apparently his luck hasn't changed.

* * *

Fuck him! Fuck them all! Yeah, maybe I'm a little drunk right now, but Takashi can just piss off! It's not my fault the pirates came here, not my fault they won, if I hadn't surrendered they would have killed me and all of us, and who does he think he is blaming me? I'm not meant to be a hero. I just want to do my job. Whether I'm doing it for the captain or….

Oh, the captain. I miss him. He was a good one, he had the best stories of times before. Back on Earth, the amazement people had as they heard about the new colonies being established, the always slightly exaggerated wonders of space. Now it's all gone to shit! No, no, just normal life. Life goes on, even with pirates. The captain, though, the captain, he was with the *Hispaniola* from the beginning too, with me. He could have done anything, he chose to captain this ship, and I let him down. Maybe Takashi is right. The captain's stories, right … my favorite was the one where he needed to do a sales pitch for a new colony, they wanted ten thousand people to go over to start it up. So he's there telling everyone how great life is there and how they can escape the crowded confines of Earth, and this guy walks in and tries to shout him down. He stands up as tall as he can—he was human then of course—and he points to the guy and says, "Best of all, he won't be there!" Everyone laughs and there's a rush of people to the front to sign up, the heckler ignored, not even forced to leave. Ah humanity, got to love 'em.

Then there was the time we were on Nova Terra—or was it Helios, they all blur together now—getting the info dump to deliver, um, who knows now, but we were going somewhere. Of course we were. And in on a shuttle comes the president of Helios—yeah, I think that was it, maybe Nova Terra though—he's requesting asylum. Apparently, a little too much of the taxes ended up in his account and people weren't too fond of that. Well, on a ship the captain—human or em—is god, if cap let him on board he'd be safe from the ravening hordes, at least until we delivered him somewhere. But he knew he couldn't force his way on; if he came against the captain's wishes, he'd have nowhere to hide. So we listened to him beg, plead for his life, promise the captain—and all of us—riches, probably from his ill-gotten gains but he didn't emphasize that part. If the captain had had a face it would have been stony, as he saw several other shuttles coming up, ordering the president to surrender. Captain never let him in, told him it was his people he had crossed, now he had to face them himself.

Oh, captain! I'm sorry I let you down. Could I have been as strong as you? I thought I did the right thing! Maybe when I'm sober I'll feel better about it again. Stupid Takashi! Getting me all worked up. What'd he have to go and do that for? Like he really would have kept fighting to the end. Pshaw! Takashi has never had a fight in his life. Well, not that I really know. Maybe there's more there than I know. No, he's just being an asshole. Fuck him. I was right, it needed to be done. And we'll be fine with the pirates now, who cares that they're pirates anyway? We just do our jobs, just follow orders. That's right, that's what we do. Okay, enough drunken reverie now, good night.

Chapter 8

A quiet ping was emitted from Sybil's suspension pod as it began the process of waking her. She had spent the last thirty years waiting for a reply to her message; that was part of the deal—the upfront payment included enough to cover rent and power for the duration, but apparently Phoenix didn't want her risking herself in any other activities until his job was complete. A slight vapor started to form around the pod as the internal temperature heated up to 37 degrees. Electrical and chemical stimuli that had kept her body in suspended animation, barely aging a day the entire time she was in there, started to run faster and bring her heart rate up to normal speed. Finally, after an hour, her eyes opened, and she was able to wiggle her fingers and stretch her arm up to push the release button. The pod door slid aside, and she stepped out once again into her room, unchanged from when she had last seen it but for a thin layer of dust that had settled during the years she had been asleep.

After getting up, she immediately went to the terminal. She had kept an em running to make any necessary software updates, so the terminal would remain compatible with any technology changes that came along while she was in suspension. Not that she had expected much in thirty years, but if all went according to plan she would have an even longer sleep ahead of her. From her em she learned that in fact only one minor upgrade had been required; it might be interesting for her to learn about it, but it probably wouldn't be worthwhile if she just had to return to her pod. Then she saw the message she had been waiting for, the one that had triggered her suspension pod to wake her, received on the university's gravitational wave detector and routed to her terminal, with the anomaly deleted from the detector's logs, of course. "On my way." Only three words, and a UBC blockchain for the next portion of her payment. This alone would allow her to live as she dreamed for the rest of her natural life—in fact, rather beyond her natural life. But she wasn't just in it for the money; this was what she had signed up for, a huge challenge, and she wouldn't trade the excitement of the hack for anything.

Now she had a little preparation to do. Calculating the round-trip time from when she had sent her message to receiving the reply, she was able to estimate how far out Phoenix's ship was. Exactly how fast it would be traveling she didn't know, of course, but like most ships, it would probably be cruising around one-tenth the speed of light, so she could get a rough estimate of arrival time. She checked the port logs for planned arrivals, which were published well in advance; even though there could be a high margin of error this far out, people other than Sybil would still want to plan for them, so she didn't even have to resort to hacking tricks to get it. There it was, a mail ship from New Jupiter due from that direction in 108 years. She looked up the specs on the ship—cruising speed, acceleration, deceleration—then calculated how far out it would be now based on its estimated time of arrival. It lined up perfectly with what she had calculated based on the round trip time of her message. That was way too far in the future for her to get anything started now, though. She programmed her pod to wake her one year before the ship's arrival, which would give her plenty of time to have everything prepared, and she set her em to monitor the mail ship's arrival time—as it got closer its transmissions would help the port adjust the ETA—and wake her early if needed.

She decided to go on one last run before re-entering the pod; her muscles would, of course, be stimulated the whole time she was in there, but it still seemed like stretching her legs would be a good idea before a hundred year sleep. Plus she had a craving for a chocolate bar, and she hadn't kept any food around her apartment, knowing it would go stale or worse. She laced up her shoes and headed down toward the beach. The sun was just starting to set, and as she ran along the beach the whole spectrum of colors shifted through the sky. She loved listening to the waves breaking gently offshore, the gulls crying out overhead, and the occasional children laughing as she ran by them. It sure didn't feel to her like thirty years had passed; sure, if she went into the city she would have noticed changes, but the beach here was timeless. She picked up her pace a little, starting to break a sweat.

Ahead of her the cliffs jutted out to a point, narrowing the beach and at high tide separating it into two sections. The tide was out now, though, so she was able to stay on the beach around the point, rather than taking the trail up and over it. As she passed the point, she glanced up and saw a man in a dark coat with binoculars. Oddly, the binoculars weren't aimed out toward the sea; instead, he was looking down at the beach, right where she was running. Well, she was still young, and good looking—at least she thought so, athletic body, dark skin, and cropped black hair, almost boyish but with enough curves to give away that game —and this wouldn't be the first time a guy had checked her out; it still seemed weird though. When she got to the end of the beach, she looked back toward the point; he seemed to still be looking at her, but it was hard to tell from that distance in the fading light. Rather than returning along the beach, she turned toward the street, to come up behind the strange man. But when she got back to where she had seen him, the space was empty. He must have left when a building or car—or something—had been blocking her view. There had been plenty of time for him to go, after all, and the sun had set, so many people had left already or were in the process of walking away from the beach. Maybe she had been imagining it in the first place; maybe he had just tilted his head down to scratch his neck while she happened to pass by. Maybe she should have stayed home and just gotten back into her pod; no—she loved running too much, it was worth being stared at a little by some freak. Still, it was creepy enough to make her run faster, looking carefully at every doorway and alley she went past—there! no, just a shadow—and maybe she would need to stick to daylight runs after she woke up from the suspension pod again. It was clearly too much to hope for that in a hundred years all the creepy guys would be gone.

She reached her front door and went inside. "Damn! I forgot the chocolate." She must have been more flustered than she realized by the peeping tom. But it was dark now, and there was no way she was going back out tonight. Besides, the pod was waiting for her; too much longer and it might time out, and it would be a hassle to have to reconfigure it. Still, she needed a quick shower—100-year old sweat would not feel too good when she woke up. As she waited for the water to warm up, she noticed another message coming in for her, appearing to be from the same gravitational wave channel that she had used to communicate with Phoenix. But that was supposed to have been a one-time program, deleting itself along with any artifacts of the communication as soon as the message was received. Had Phoenix sent a second message before her program had completely shut down? She opened up the new arrival; it was just a series of 8s. That didn't make any sense to her—what would Phoenix mean by that? Or had somebody overridden her hack in order to insert that message? If that was the case, what would it mean? A warning? Not a very good one, if she couldn't figure out what she was being warned about. A directive? Just as bad, if she didn't know what it meant for her to do. A troll of some kind, just to make her paranoid? Maybe not even with that intent, but some other hacker who got into the gravity wave system for some reason—

it hadn't been that hard for her after all—saw her hack, and wrote one on top of it. Yeah, that was most likely it, someone just showing off to get his name out there, not having any idea what she was using it for; luckily, whoever had done it hadn't erased her receiver entirely, or she would never have gotten Phoenix's message. She was just feeling paranoid because of the run; there would be no need to worry about this person, who would probably be long gone by the time she woke up anyway.

Feeling better by the end of her shower that the message was meaningless, she climbed back into the suspension pod, closed the door, and closed her eyes. As the temperature fell, and her brain activity along with it, she thought she remembered where she had seen a man like that before, but she was out before it fully clicked into place.

Chapter 9

erne reached the space elevator portal, all glass and carbon fiber, what on pre-Space Age Earth would have been called very modern architecture. It was a huge contrast to the stone castle of a lodge where he had spent most of his time on Jurassia, and even more so compared to the meager tents he would stay in when clients signed up for long-term expeditions.

Inside, the portal was very similar to an airport, whether on Jurassia, Earth, or any other planet. Those who hadn't arranged for a ship yet could find a listing of upcoming departures. A similar listing showed ships that were expected to arrive. The arrival board could be interesting; a ship that was scheduled to arrive today may now be showing an arrival time several years away based on the most recent signals received from the ship. Worse were the ones expected to arrive months ago but with no arrival time listed; most likely those had met some accident and their fate would never be known, but traditionally they were left on the board for at least a year, just in case they were still en route but unable to communicate.

For those uninterested in interstellar travel, there were

other options. Orbital shuttles left the top of the elevator regularly, giving tourists the experience of freefall for a few hours and an "out of this world" view (as the cliché-prone advertisements put it). Jurassia had a small station in permanent orbit, which supported scientific research but also the occasional visitor looking for a change of scenery. Even the elevator itself was a destination of sorts, and families could often be seen riding up and down, a two-week vacation that would fill their children's eyes with wonder.

The port had little in the way of security, at least of the intrusive variety. Security ems and human experts monitored video and chemical feeds constantly—not just in the port itself but through enough of the surrounding area that a troublemaker would be highly unlikely to get to the elevator without being arrested first. The elevator itself was highly resistant to sabotage. It had to be, and not only to protect against human attacks; with so many things that could go wrong just from the whims of nature, redundancy and self-healing were not optional.

Herne, of course, had his ticket, had in fact been preparing for this trip for a long time. He dropped his baggage off on a conveyor. Though he would be away for centuries, possibly never returning, he brought only the minimal personal belongings, mostly things with sentimental value—a photo of Allison, a tooth from his first allosaurus kill, and the totems that he had kept from his childhood. Anything large was far too expensive to transport between systems, and could be easily be created (or recreated with the design files he carried on his safedisk) on a printer when he arrived at his destination. Most of the goods in his rooms had belonged to the lodge, and the rest he left for the owner to dispose of—Owen had sure looked pleased when he saw some of the hunting trophies that Herne was leaving behind.

Leaving the baggage conveyor, he walked toward the elevator, eventually reaching the doors to the elevator car itself. After scanning his ticket and his iris to confirm his identity, he was able to enter and find his seat. When he had arrived at Jurassia he had taken the cheapest seat available, cramped between other passengers, very uncomfortable for a five-day journey, especially for a man of his height. Now, although he had proven himself capable of handling even more severe discomfort on some of his outings, he needed to prepare himself for the Pilgrimage, so he had reserved a private compartment. That would allow him to recline when tired and begin the contemplation rituals without distraction or disturbance. But first, he ordered a bottle of wine and a nice steak—imported beef from another settlement in the system, not stegosaurus—thinking that would be a great beginning for the trip.

* * *

Five days later, after a relaxing and entertaining trip, Herne reached the top of the elevator. The top portal wasn't much different in appearance than the ground one, though gravity was much lower. Herne could recognize the frequent travelers; they were the ones who didn't need to hold the handrails just to keep from flying across the room every time they took a simple step. Of course, it had been so long since he had been up there that he was slightly embarrassed to realize this time he would be one of the handrail-holders, at least until he got his space legs back under him. But he was in no hurry, so he could take his time getting to the shuttle that would take him to his final spaceship, settled in a more distant orbit.

He was barely out of his elevator car, though, when a security guard came up to him and asked him politely to follow. Herne was surprised, to say the least—he knew poachers would occasionally try to take dinosaur eggs off the planet, but all his artifacts were legal and carried openly so scanners should have picked up anything problematic on the ground, where he would have happily, or at least willingly, given them up if asked. But he allowed the guard to escort him, curious as much as anything else to see what might come of this.

The security guard took him to an unmarked office door, knocked briefly, and opened the door for Herne. He entered cautiously, expecting the guard to follow, but instead the guard simply closed the door, and the sound of footsteps made Herne even more puzzled since, apparently, the guard wasn't even making sure he stayed. The puzzlement didn't last long, though, as Herne heard a loud voice bellow, "Herne Sutherland!"

Turning, Herne saw a man as large as himself, with white hair and a trimmed beard, who he instantly recognized. "Magellan! How have you been?"

"Fine, fine. Have a seat." Herne stretched out on a plush faux leather couch while Magellan pulled his chair around from behind an enormous desk, empty but for an embedded terminal screen which was almost invisible as the wood grain on the display did its best to match the rest of the surface. "So you've finally had enough of us, have you?" Magellan smirked and continued, "We've tried so hard to get rid of you...."

"Ha! If you'd really been trying, you know I'd stay just to spite you." Herne returned the smirk and looked around at the walls filled with bookshelves, some of the books looking like they were old enough to have been on the original colonization ships from Earth. This looked more like a private study or library than an actual office, and Herne realized that was probably what it was, given the lack of any official identification on the door or desk. "What have they got you doing these days? I thought you were running the station."

"Has it really been that long since you've seen me?"

"Three years."

"And you've not been paying attention to the news at all?"

"Well, you know what they say, no news is good news. So, what, my old hunting buddy got kicked out? They caught you drinking too much? You never could hold your liquor...."

"I remember a few nights when you were under the table, young man. But no, if you really don't know, I was elected last year as magistrate of the system."

"Damn! How did I not know that? Sorry, sir." The last was said with a completely straight face.

"Don't you 'sir' me, Herne," Magellan said as Herne broke into a smile. "Honestly, don't. I get enough of that shit, I don't need it from you."

"So to what do I owe this great honor, noble magistrate?"

"Seriously, stop it! Since you obviously don't follow even the most basic news, you probably don't even know about the pirate problem."

"Oh yeah, I do. They were a risk back before I came here."

"Yeah, well, if anything it has gotten worse. An inbound ship was hijacked or destroyed just before I took office—or at least that's when we got the emergency message it broadcast as the attack started. It was still two light years out, and we heard nothing more from it since. And another ship arrived last week having narrowly evaded capture en route."

"Still, that's only two out of hundreds of ships going in and out every year. Sure it's a risk, but there are plenty of other risks to space travel. If you're trying to stop me from leaving, you'll have to do better than that. Try itinerant black holes, maybe."

"Dude, you hunt dinosaurs for a living. I know you're not afraid of risks, and I wouldn't waste my time coming here just to tell you to be careful. No, what I'm looking for—and I'm hoping other systems will follow my lead or have already thought of it themselves—I'm asking you to take on the responsibility of pirate hunter. Kind of like the old privateers. There are two systems—Corsa and Barbary—that I suspect are launching these pirates...."

"Did you say Corsa? I thought that was one of the mythical slave planets."

"No, Corsa's a real system. Whether they actually use

slaves, I can't say for sure, but some evidence I've received from other systems suggests it's likely. But whether they keep the slaves or not, they are definitely supporting pirate attacks on interstellar ships."

"Definitely? How do you know?"

"I got a message last week from Corsa. A request for ransom."

"To you as system magistrate? Did they kidnap some sort of diplomat?"

"No, to me personally. You never knew my brother; he was much older than me. I grew up playing with his children, had lots of fun with my cousins Fay and Francis, until my brother decided to move his family to another system. I was about thirteen at the time, I didn't understand the reasons, got angry and said some things I probably shouldn't have, but only because I knew I would miss them. And I did miss them, for a very long time. But life goes on. Until last week, when I heard that they had been kidnapped."

"Shit! No! All of them?"

"No, that's the worst part. Just my brother and his wife. No mention of the kids at all. So are they dead? Do the pirates just assume they're not valuable? I have no idea, and I probably won't for several more years—decades, really—until I can get a response. And that makes it harder—if I pay the ransom now, they'll know I'm willing, and they'll probably charge even more for the kids, never mind how much extra time they'd have to wait before they'd be freed, and who knows if they're keeping them in suspension or letting them age, working them to death maybe before I even get an opportunity to rescue them. I mean, shit! Of course I'm going to ransom my brother; I just wish I could save them all now!"

Herne didn't know what to say. He was never good at these emotional moments, so he stood up and silently put his arm around Magellan, waiting for him to finish crying. At least he knew why Magellan had chosen this room rather than his regular office in a busier part of the terminal.

"So pirate hunter, eh? What does that actually mean?"

"Sorry," he sniffed. "You'd have authorization from me, as Jurassia system magistrate, to attack any Corsan or Barbary ships you come across in your travels. Don't worry, you don't have to stay awake for the whole trip—your ship will be programmed to detect them and wake you if needed. And speaking of your ship, I've got one for you, decked out with all the weapons you may need—hydrogen bombs, neutron bombs, EMPs, you name it—fully shielded and faster than the commercial transport you were planning to use. I'll make sure the Olympia magistrate knows of your commission, in case any complaints reach there, and I'll give you a safedisk with the same information—your very own 'letters of marque'—in case you end up in another system or the direct message doesn't get received."

"And if I don't want to?"

"Well, you don't have to do anything. Any engagement is entirely up to you. All I'm giving you is legal protection in case something goes wrong in your efforts. But I would expect any pirates that were, shall we say, no longer a threat to civilized systems would lead to great rewards for whoever caused their demise."

"All right. No promises—you know I'm heading there for the Pilgrimage."

"I know."

"And I need to be in the right state of mind for that. Attacking pirates is not quite the thing for a pilgrim."

"Just keep an eye out. Even after your Pilgrimage, your commission will be valid, and I doubt all pirates everywhere will be defeated before then."

"No," Herne laughed, "I suppose not."

"By the way, I am glad to see you doing the Pilgrimage. I had a chance to ten years ago and turned it down, and I regret it. Too many responsibilities now, but perhaps another chance will come before it's too late for me."

"Oh come on, you're not that old. I'll leave a cup there for you, for when you follow me."

"Now it is you who does me the great honor." Magellan smiled. "Anyway, safe travels, here's your safedisk. I'm glad to have known you, Herne, and perhaps if you return here you can take my great-great grandkids hunting."

"I will, I will. Take care, Magellan. I know the system is in good hands with you."

With that, Herne opened the door and walked back into the hallway. "Pirate hunter, hmmm...," he mumbled under his breath. Maybe not quite as thrilling as dinosaurs. No, not at all, since the odds of him actually meeting a pirate were so slim, he didn't know why Magellan had even bothered, though he figured a politician has to look like he's doing something and handing out pirate hunting licenses is definitely something.

The rest of the walk to the shuttle was uninterrupted, and two hours later Herne got his first glimpse of what would be his ship. It was a beauty, one of the nicest he had ever even seen, and definitely the nicest he had ever actually been on. Sleek, almost aerodynamic, not that he intended to take it through atmosphere—taking an interstellar ship up and down a major gravity well took too much energy—but the ship designers obviously wanted it to be prepared for anything. Not much of a gyro section, it would be tight even for one person, and it certainly wouldn't take much of a crew. But the way Magellan had described it he was sure it would have top notch ems running all the systems. A spherical area in the center housed the fusion drive, bulging out beyond the gyro ring, allowing it to direct its thrust in any direction. Weapons ports spread around the gyro. This was truly a warship, and now it was his warship. Make that his pirate hunting ship, he thought with a grin.

The shuttle docked with the ship, and inside was just as impressive as out. Everything looked brand new, metal surfaces still gleaming, walkways well lit, control panels waiting for use. And it was more spacious than he had expected based on the exterior. Sure, he would spend most of his time asleep in a suspension pod, but for the times when he was awake, he was going to be comfortable. Large screens displayed the system status and external views. The ems were everything he could hope for, greeting him as he entered the control room.

"Navigation?"

"Route prepared for Olympia system. We will pass through the Dyson shield at port 3, then dock at the Olympia elevator itself."

"Engineering?"

"All systems ready. Fusion drive at full potential, but we'll run at 50% this time."

"Weapons?"

"Pirates better watch out, sir!"

Herne laughed. It was good to have an em with a sense of humor, though he still doubted he would actually encounter any pirates on this trip. He strapped himself into his seat—the suspension pod would come later—and gave the order to leave. The screen in front of him showed him one last view of Jurassia, so different from this altitude; even if he had been looking through a window it would have had none of the smells and sounds that made it seem real. But it had been his home, and he would miss it, and just perhaps he would be back here some day, find a new favorite trike, and go riding out hunting allos and tyros again.

Chapter 10

One light year out from Olympia, and we received the first identification request from them, right on schedule. All crew members have been told in no uncertain terms to do nothing to give away Phoenix's presence on board, under risk of immediate termination. Pirate ems are monitoring all activity closely, no doubt about that, but most of the old communications crew are still running, and they followed instructions closely, identifying the *Hispaniola* as an information cargo ship with a handful of passengers, standard procedure every time we approached a new planet. It may be two years before we learn if the Olympia system has any suspicions, but it's unlikely they would. We're still too far out for them to detect the attached ship. It is interesting that the communications ems were told explicitly not to mention it because it will raise questions when it is noticed—what are we doing with the extra mass, which would have little value as scrap? If it's not scrap, what is in it? And why did we not mention it, are we hiding something? All questions I imagine Phoenix would not want to be asked.

* * *

There was some interesting activity near the dock today, though I can't say exactly what it is. All I know is that the doors nearest the dock have been sealed, and all sensors within that perimeter have been deactivated, so none of the crew can see what might be going on. How they managed to do that is beyond me; apparently, I'm not the best engineer on this ship anymore. Maybe I can learn something from them; that would make the hijacking worthwhile for me, anyway. And it would give me something to respond with when Takashi tries to give me a hard time for surrendering. Not that I think they would teach me anything; pirates don't have a reputation for being helpful like that. Of course, all network activity continues to be blocked by the strongest security ems I have ever encountered.

Oh. As I write this, external sensors have detected the pirate ship floating alongside us, so Phoenix must have ejected it. I wonder if it will end up in an eccentric orbit we'll intercept later, or if it will just be left to float off into space. I guess time will tell. I have no idea why we kept it for so long. I suppose there must have been something valuable on board that they wanted to offload as late as possible; the security measures prevent me from finding out what, though. There are still six months before we expect any response to our initial identification beacon, and ten years before we actually reach the system.

* * *

I was directed to adjust the suspension pods on our human passengers today, keeping them asleep long after we will arrive at Olympia. Normal operating procedure would have them wake up before arrival, to be able to identify themselves and prepare their contacts in the local system. I'm not sure how we'll get around that, but Phoenix must have a plan. At least they still seem safe and in good condition, oblivious to the change in command. I hope I never get an order to disable the pods. I'm still a human mind, after all, with the normal taboos against murder—you're not going to see me turn pirate any-time soon—but also the normal instinct toward self-preserva-tion. So if it came down to killing the passengers or being terminated myself, I don't know what I'd do. Surrendering is one thing—I'm sure I saved more lives by doing so, not just my own but others, by starting the cascade. If I had thought other-wise, … I don't know, I like to believe I would have kept fight-ing, but you never can really know until you're faced with it. Like I said, I hope I never get that order.

* * *

There's so much going on now, I haven't had much time for my journal. I have never seen a Dyson sphere this closely before. It's surprisingly black—I mean space is black, but there are always stars, nebulae, distant galaxies filling the void. But at this distance, the sphere fills nearly all of the forward field of view on our ship, and of course, it's designed to emit as little radiation as possible, keeping energy inside the system. Hence black. As these things tend to be, it's a bit of a mish-mash. Large sections of a solid shell, where most of the operations staff and communications equipment are located, with a swarm of tethered satellites giving it enough overall flexibility to handle the pressures of encompassing an entire solar system. We're heading toward one of those mini-swarms, expecting the controllers to open a passageway so we can continue toward the planets inside. Communications with the sphere are practically real-time now—still several minutes round trip delay, but shrinking rapidly.

I've learned a little about the pirates' plant inside the system. She goes by Sybil, and apparently she was in suspension until about a year ago. It's not clear exactly where she is, in the shell control station or operating remotely; she doesn't seem to actually be part of the system staff, but she somehow manages to make things happen as we need them. I don't think we could have held up the charade this long without her. As long as we were still approaching from a distance, we were fine; even up close, there is nothing external to suggest we are anything other than what we were when we left New Jupiter. But when they asked to speak to the captain, there was much commotion among the pirates; after all, none of them could access the captain's encryption keys. I noticed a side communication channel being opened that wasn't answered by the control center—later I figured out this was Sybil—and shortly afterward the control operator acknowledged that the captain's signature had been verified, even though we had never actually sent it. So now the Olympians think they are talking to the legitimate captain of our ship.

The expected inquiries about the passengers never happened either. As part of my engineering checks on the comm systems, I slipped a request for remote logs into the communication channel—not giving anything away about our ship, so it didn't attract the attention of the pirates—and I saw that all the passengers were marked as identification complete. Presumably, that was Sybil's work, too, though I'm not sure whether we passed on the identification information for her to load in the system or if she fabricated data herself. If it's the latter, that will be their problem to deal with when they do wake up, and they should be grateful that they wake up at all. All the other arrangements have been worked out—where and when to pass through the sphere, ship's mass so they can accommodate it—so there is nothing stopping us from entering the Olympia system now.

* * *

Today we reached the swarm, each satellite like a little black sea urchin, sprouting electrostatic field sensors to keep a safe distance from its neighbors, along with optical and radio interfaces to communicate with other satellites in the swarm as well as the central controller. Fascinating, then, watching the passage open. It looks like we are heading straight into the satellites, but just before we hit them they move out of the way, dancing an intricate quadrille to avoid crashing into each other as well, and falling in right behind us so that it's more like moving in a bubble than through a tunnel. A bubble that you realize could collapse and crush you at any moment if it knew you were harboring pirates. Or maybe not; it's hard to say whether the pressure from the swarm of satellites would actually be enough to overcome our repeller shields, or if we could blast our way out if necessary. Regardless, it's enough to make even an em feel claustrophobic, and we came close to finding out. Halfway through—well, somewhere in the middle, I wasn't tracking exactly how far we had gone—the satellite straight ahead of us wasn't moving. Navigation gave orders for hard deceleration, our nose stopping about a kilometer away from it. Everyone was worried—were we stuck here? were we caught? Communications was absolutely forbidden from hailing the control center; if there were any questions about us, Phoenix didn't want any information leaking out that might confirm their suspicions. Weapons were activated and ready, in case it did come to that. And my team looked closely at all the sensors and monitors to see if we could figure out what was going on. There was nothing obvious, but it looked like one of the satellites behind us wasn't falling back into place, and we thought that failure might be preventing the others from following it. We had a maintenance arm sticking out that way, not far enough that it would be interfering with the satellites, and we had gotten this far without any problem, but if the stuck satellite's sensors were misaligned a bit, maybe it would think the arm was in its way. So I reoriented it, more straight across our stern. That seemed to do the trick; the satellite behind us started moving back into place, the others following it, and the space ahead of us clearing once again. Slowly, in case it wasn't going to last, we started moving ahead, but the rest of the passage was uneventful.

Aside from the vulnerability to failures like that, you would think the energy required for all this motion and coordination would be more than what would be lost through a straightforward gap in the shell. Maybe it is; maybe there are other reasons for it—security or simply to show off their technology. Anyway, we are through now, apparently with no one aware of who is at our helm (except Sybil, of course) and no ultimate test of ship versus swarm. The planets of the system are visible ahead of us, the outer planets with their rings, and Olympia itself glowing even at this distance, its intense energy use typical for a civilized planet of its size, but still much more than what I was used to in most of my life on Earth. At least the way I remember Earth; it's quite possible I'm idealizing it, thinking of it as some ancient pre-modern culture compared to the civilization spreading around the galaxy now, and maybe it wasn't actually so different. How strange not to see stars, though, just reflections of the sun from the interior of the Dyson sphere. Especially at the end of an interstellar journey when stars were all there was to see for so long. (And when you did see something else, it was usually something bad, like, say, a pirate ship!)

Chapter 11

With Phoenix's ship through the Dyson sphere, the first part of Sybil's work was complete. In truth, it had not been hard. Most of the control station was run by humans, who are easily distracted and forgetful. As soon as she had woken from the suspension pod—which had happened right on time, her calculation of the ship's arrival time perfect—she had set to work on creating a back door into the incoming ship record database. With a year to do this, she was in no hurry. The first six months were spent coming up to speed on the latest technological changes that happened while she slept. It amazed her how such things went in cycles; if she had been awake the whole time she would have spent far too much time learning different paradigms only to end up back where she had started. The details still changed, of course, but there were immersion courses for teaching new arrivals from other systems, who would face the same problem she did, and she was a very fast learner.

Once she had become an expert in the latest protocols, or as expert as one could be in half a year, she started probing for weaknesses in the control network. She knew there was bound to be one; over a thousand years of interstellar expansion, and humanity still had not managed to create a perfectly secure communication system. She was able to take advantage of the multi-hour latency between Olympia and the Dyson sphere and found a flaw in how the network timing handled this, and within weeks she had the back door that she needed. Throughout this time, she was keeping up her running, but more cautiously now. The man she had seen when she was running during her brief interval awake had spooked her, and she now remembered seeing a similar man at the bar when she had seduced the postdoc into handing her the password to the gravity wave detector. Now, whenever she went out, she seemed to see him again, always out of the corner of her eye, but when she would turn there would be no sign of him. Paranoia, obviously; he couldn't still be following her after more than a hundred years, could he? But she couldn't shake the feeling, so gradually she had stopped leaving her apartment other than for her runs.

With a live feed of the communication stream between the *Hispaniola* and the sphere control station, and access to the incoming ship records, she was able to take advantage of the communication delays to insert spoofed data. Then when the traffic controllers went to check for a response from the ship, they would see the data was already there. So they would assume they had miscalculated the timing, or maybe forgotten and asked for the same thing twice; they were busy with other ships too, so slips like that were understandable, and the data was there, so it must have come from the ship, right? She only had to do that a few times, confusing a different controller each time, who of course wouldn't want to admit their mistake to the others, so there was never a pattern for them to detect. Someday they would delegate this job to ems, and she would have to resort to other tricks, but people in the Olympia system were very traditional, preferring human labor whenever possible, not only for functions related to the Pilgrimage.

The next stage was even simpler; with Phoenix's ship inside the Dyson sphere, she could use a direct communication link to guide the ship exactly to its destination, the asteroid Eleusis. It wasn't quite as simple as plugging coordinates into a navigation device; the ship could have done those calculations itself. The *Hispaniola* was supposed to stop at the L2 Lagrange point for Olympia, where it could transfer its information and passengers, who were expected to be out of suspension already, to a shuttle bound for the Olympia space elevator. If Phoenix headed straight for Eleusis, the diversion would quickly be detected. But she had come up with a plan to get the ship in the right place at the right time, able to land directly on the asteroid without notice, while appearing on its reported course as long as possible. It would start with a detour through the outer planets.

"Burn thrusters 2 and 3 at half power for 30 seconds. If anyone asks, your passengers wanted to pass through Roma's rings. It's common enough that I doubt anyone will bother to ask."

"Perfect, but actually through the rings?"

"Yes, it's a thing. They're sparse enough here, it's actually quite safe."

"I trust you. You've gotten us this far."

That she had. And with the bitcoin transfer after Phoenix got through the sphere, she really would never have to work again. More importantly, this was a unique challenge for her, trying to visualize trajectories in her head, or on her terminal screen when they got too complicated, rather than her usual social engineering and probing for information security weaknesses. In a way, though, this was just social engineering on a large scale, making everything seem harmless to anyone who might be watching while really setting up for the big score later.

Getting Phoenix on the right trajectory was not all that was needed, though. She needed to make sure no one started paying attention to the ship on the strange path. Sure, a brief detour to Roma wasn't out of the ordinary, and neither were any of the other steps she would have him go through. But add them all up? For passengers that had been traveling all the way from New Jupiter and probably would be eager to get established on their new home, or started on their Pilgrimage if that was the reason for their journey? It would be odd to say the least. So she monitored network traffic, official logs, small talk throughout the city, listening and watching for anyone that might be noticing the *Hispaniola*. Unfortunately this required her getting out of the house, which made her increasingly uncomfortable. She had even cut back her runs to twice a week, because every time she went, she felt like she had a shadow pacing behind her. Still nothing tangible, though, and she kept telling herself it was all in her head, getting even more angry at that one creep who had made her so paranoid. But she had to be out there, listening, and every time she heard something, the person involved would get fired, or win an off-planet vacation, or end up in a coma due to an industrial accident (news reports were excited about that one, as machinery had not gone so berserk in the history of the city). And then there were the conspiracy theorists who might notice all these odd coincidences and put the pieces together. Luckily, they were easy to deal with: try to shut them down and it would only make them more paranoid, but feed them even more information, mostly false of course, and they would build up their imagined conspiracy to such complexity that no one would ever believe them. It drove some of them crazy, and she could only imagine how they would feel if they knew that this conspiracy theory of theirs was actually true!

All the while, she tried to ease her own paranoia by setting up a fail-safe system, so if something were to happen to her, at least Phoenix would have some protection. It wasn't just out of loyalty, of course; if she did get in trouble, Phoenix was really the only one who might be able to help her get out. It wasn't a guarantee, since she wouldn't be able to send a message about what had happened, but it was at least a chance. She had a database of all ships currently at Olympia—no hacking even required for that one, as it was public information. And she had operational instructions for all their navigation and communication systems; that was … not exactly public, but readily available if one knew where to look, and she had plenty of connections in that shadow network. One ship at a time, she slipped in a little bit of obfuscation that could be triggered if necessary, nothing that anyone would notice until it was necessary.

It didn't help her paranoia, though. Or it helped only in the sense that it kept her fear from getting worse, every bit of safety she felt as she developed her fail-safe counteracting the additional worry from another day of being here on Olympia, visible, and possibly watched. But it was all she could do. Her home security was already state of the art; she had body implants and smart clothing that would help her in a pinch; and she really was the best at what she was doing, so why was she so worried?

After two months of this, her plan was working perfectly. A loop through the outer planets had brought Phoenix's ship in a straight line with both the L2 point and Eleusis. Now it would be passing behind Eleusis, disappearing momentarily from the sight of anyone watching on Olympia, making it the perfect time to make the move. She already had the comm link up and ready.

"Hard deceleration burn on my mark.... Now!"

"Done."

"Now you should be falling to Eleusis, 30 kilometers from the Pilgrimage entrance. I won't be able to see fine enough details to aid you, so landing is all yours."

"Thank you for your help, Sybil. I hope you have found this rewarding."

"Absolutely. Need any help again, look me up."

And with that, she stood up from her terminal, stretched, and shook her head, her mind finally free to think about something other than the Phoenix job. She wondered again what Phoenix was there for. She wasn't religious at all, and didn't care what happened to the Pilgrimage site, but it seemed an odd place for pirates to visit. Could they be stealing artifacts for ransom? Perhaps, and certainly the Nupists would pay a lot to recover them, probably even enough to cover all the money she had been paid. But still, why? What would Phoenix do with the payment? Wasn't it easier just to stick to open space, hijacking ships like most pirates did? Maybe, like her, they were doing this precisely because it wasn't easier, she thought with a grin. Anyway, it wasn't her problem anymore; now it was time to go for another run and then figure out what system to head to next, where she could find some new marks.

Chapter 12

It was Herne's first time passing through a Dyson sphere also Jurassia didn't need one; with the major settled planet operating as a wildlife refuge with low population, the energy needs of the minor planetary colonies, asteroids, and stations could be met by local fusion and solar flux. The system he had been born in had been starting to build one at the time he left; it was probably complete by now, given the centuries that had passed as he traveled, but he never expected to return. He had left his family on poor terms, an angry, rebellious young man wanting a more adventurous life than they could offer him.

Looking back, he wished he had handled it better; there had been no need for yelling, for hateful words aimed at people who only wanted the best for him, even if they didn't really understand what he needed. But he needed to leave, would have been miserable confined in the city, while his parents couldn't conceive of a life away from what was familiar to them, had probably never even traveled more than a hundred kilometers from their home. Of course, even if he were to return, they would be long dead; Herne had had no siblings, but even if there were still distant cousins of his in the system, he didn't expect any stories of himself to have been passed down through the generations.

When Herne saw the swarm of satellites moving apart and filling in behind his ship, he was reminded of the graceful motion of a herd of hadrosaurs running through the marshes. Seen from a distance it was a smooth wave, like gently stirring coloring into liquid. Up close, and he had seen it very up close, it was chaotic, and yet somehow they all managed to coordinate, to not trip or collide into one another. Herne kept expecting every moment the system to fall apart, with a single mistake cascading through the entire herd, but it never happened.

The trip up to that point had been uneventful, with Herne waking up as scheduled to see the sights, then returning to his suspension pod. No pirates, despite Magellan's worries, and Herne rolled his eyes remembering that conversation. The Olympia system controllers had made a point of addressing him as "Pirate Hunter Herne Sutherland" as he arrived, so the notification message had gotten through, but he didn't like being treated with such honor when he hadn't done anything to earn it. Mostly, though, his thoughts here were on the Pilgrimage. He looked forward to landing on Eleusis, being surrounded by the temple cats, purchasing the ritual cups to place along the way in memory of those who had been important on his life's journey—not that the temple needed money, but the purchase was symbolic, a throwback to earlier times when people would sacrifice significant income to support their preferred religion or other groups that promised their followers peace and contentment in return. Then the labyrinth descent, choosing his path and recognizing that every pilgrim's way was unique, until finally, he would reach the Eleusinian Totem. This last part was still a mystery to him—sure, he could have found pictures of it if he had wanted, although pilgrims were forbidden from recording their Pilgrimage or speaking of the Totem in any way, but he had chosen not to look, the anticipation being an important part of the preparation for him.

But all that was still weeks ahead. First, he had to rendezvous at the planet Olympia, and when his ship reached the Lagrange point, he left it and took a shuttle to the space elevator portal. Unlike Jurassia's modern design, this elevator was architected to seem ancient, even though it was built with the same underlying technology. Every face had a different appearance; one looked like the entrance to a Haida longhouse, with totems of orca, eagle, and bear, another a Shinto shrine, with a great Torii gate to pass through (not exactly under, depending on the gravity perspective of the arriving spacecraft), a third a great pyramid, flanked by Sphinx. Herne's shuttle docked among great Ionic pillars, adorned with "carvings" (actually, as he knew, shaped carbon fiber) of grape vines and centaurs. As he passed through the airlock he was welcomed by statues of Hermes and Athena, with actual olive trees lining the corridor. Herne appreciated the effort, but he was soon confronted by the unpleasant reality of interstellar travel: quarantine. There was a huge risk of differential evolution of microorganisms across systems. And while most interstellar ships carried samples of antibiotics and antivirals that were adapted to the germs at their source, along with detailed genetic information, pathology reports, and molecular assembly instructions for the medicines, no system wanted to play the role of the Americas at the introduction of smallpox. So all extra-system immigrants were subject to a three-day quarantine, sufficient time for the medical information to be processed, the arrivals to be fully tested, and all internal microorganisms to be classified.

Sitting in the quarantine room, Herne was at least able to chat with other arrivals and with the doctors, even if it was less comfortable than a seat at the Jurassia bar and had to be done through terminals to avoid potential contagion. Many of the visitors were pilgrims like him, some young, some old. The one that intrigued him most had an incredible story about piracy:

"I was about twelve years old, taking a vacation with my parents and older sister. We were staying in-system, hopping from station to station, and it was one of those ships where they play with gravity just to mess with the passengers—of course, all us kids loved that kind of thing, though now it would drive me nuts. Anyway, we were passing up close to the rings of one of the outer planets, when another ship appeared on an intercept course with us. Up until then, I had enjoyed talking with the crew about their work, but once that ship appeared all the ems became unresponsive, and the humans were clearly trying to encourage the passengers, kids especially, to stay in their bunks. Two days later, I felt an explosion ripple through the ship; it had hit the front, far from the passenger rooms, and that section was quickly sealed off. Even the best attempts of the crew to keep quiet couldn't prevent the occasional whisper of 'pirate' being heard, and soon all the passengers were talking about it.

"More explosions came, but it was clear they were intended to weaken the ship, not destroy it, and soon the pirate ship had docked with us. A band of huge, muscular, sword-wielding ruffians forced their way through the airlock. Our crew did the best they could to defend us—humans sacrificing themselves to lead the invaders into sections where ems would cut off air—but the pirates were prepared for all this, even bringing their own oxygen supply, and soon all the crew was dead. Then they headed aft to the passenger quarters. As I heard them approaching our room, I jumped into our luggage trunk. My sister likewise tried to hide in the closet, but she was too late; they entered as she was closing the door, and they grabbed her and carried her out into the hallway. I heard my parents scream from their room next door, as they were taken too and saw my sister ahead of them. They never called my name, though, realizing that if I was hidden it was better not to draw attention to me.

"I stayed in that trunk in silence for twelve hours before I felt safe to emerge. I managed to get one of the ems activated, and when the pirate ship was far enough away we set off an emergency beacon. After two weeks alone, a rescue shuttle finally arrived and took me back home, but I never saw my family again."

"So … you were the sole survivor of a pirate attack?" Herne was skeptical.

"Absolutely."

"Where was this?"

"Utopia."

"Never heard of it. And how did you know about the swords and the crew's defenses if you were hiding in your room?"

"Well, I …"

"Nice story, man. Very entertaining, I appreciate it. Looks like they're coming to let me out now."

After he was released from quarantine, he proceeded to the elevator itself. Again, he had his own reserved compartment on the elevator, so he was able to spread out and relax. This time, in the compartment across the aisle, he saw a woman playing with four small kittens. Pets were extremely rare on interstellar trips; it was possible to program suspension pods for them, but since they didn't understand what was going on it was very stressful for them, and it was thought that this elevated stress led to the relatively high fatality rate. Most likely this woman was just riding the elevator up and down—as on Jurassia, this was a common trip for those who wanted to get a new perspective on the planet without having to say goodbye to their accustomed life. But it was still a first for Herne to see cats in an elevator, even outside the no-mammal zone of Jurassia.

On the way down, Herne found himself awake as the elevator passed through the stationary point. As the planet's gravity balanced out the centrifugal force on the elevator, the passengers experienced a moment of zero gravity. Looking down the aisle of the elevator car, Herne saw the different reactions this induced: those who had done this many times before, sitting strapped in, focused on whatever they were doing; those new to this, gripping on for dear life lest they launch themselves across the car and hurt themselves or someone else; and those, neither fearful nor jaded, who could still enjoy the moment, eyes lit up as they bounced around. Herne glanced over to see how the cats were handling this. The owner was holding them still, but the ball of yarn one had been playing with was floating just out of its reach, and it seemed very confused as it finally tapped it and the yarn went flying off, never coming down. Herne himself didn't care much for zero gravity, he got his excitement elsewhere, so he closed his eyes to rest some more, knowing he had a couple more days before he would finally reach the planet's surface.

When he exited the elevator at ground level, the city of Olympia opened up before him. He didn't have to come down here—he could have returned directly to his ship after quarantine—but he had decided to visit Olympia first, and he was glad he did. He had been in cities before, but the contrast to his time in Jurassia was still overwhelming. Skyscrapers towered over the streets, the different forms of architecture somehow blending into a smooth whole. Individual transport vehicles zipped around corners almost faster than Herne could see. He was going to have to be as careful here as on a dinosaur hunt at least until he got used to it.

He picked a moving walkway at random, not having anywhere in particular to go, and hopped on. He marveled at the buildings he passed by—temples to commerce, to entertainment, to knowledge. The people inside might not always think of them that way, but temples they were, and to one preparing for the Pilgrimage it was easy to see them as such. Herne wandered through the city a while, hopping from walkway to walkway as he felt the urge. As he passed one building with a sign of an ale flagon wearing a Viking helmet hanging above the door, he heard raucous laughter from inside, so he stepped off the walkway and headed inside to check it out.

A long bar filled the center of the room, and a group of men and women, probably regulars by their obvious camaraderie, sat in the middle of it. Herne called out, "Anyone need a pirate hunter?" and they all turned toward him, raised their glasses, and cheered.

"Arrr!" one slurred. "We be pirates!" And the rest of the group erupted in laughter.

"Sorry, man. No pirates here. But pull up a chair and I'll pour you a drink," said the bartender.

Herne introduced himself to the group, telling the story of how he left Jurassia. ("So apparently now I'm 'Pirate Hunter Herne!'" he finished, making them all laugh.) Then he settled in to listen to their life stories. They all seemed glad to have someone new to tell them to. Herne had been right about them being regulars; all but one of them had been born here on Olympia, and the other had come here as a child, his parents part of a great exodus from a planet that was experiencing extreme tectonic activity.

"I don't remember much. Seeing videos of lava flows covering cities, gaps in the ground opening up and swallowing others. One big earthquake hit our city, our home was undamaged but few buildings could say that. That's what finally convinced Ma to leave—Dad had been wanting to go for some time—and a week later we were on a passenger ship with at least ten thousand others, all strangers to us, pods packed probably closer than they were designed to be and no room on board for anything else. I don't know why they picked Olympia, maybe it was just the first ship they could get on. People were leaving as fast as ships could get them off. Some of them staying in-system, we had moon or asteroid settlements and a couple stations. But we were worried about overcrowding in those and figured if we have to pick up and move, we may as well go all the way. The news beat us here, of course— our city had been destroyed about four months later, millions dead who had been sure it would calm down any day now. Instead, by the time we got here, civilization on the planet was basically gone. A few nomadic tribes still survived, but everyone else had evacuated or died."

Everyone quietly raised their glasses in honor of the dead. Not all the stories were so downbeat, though. There was the woman who ran a souvenir shop at the base of the space elevator but had never been off the planet herself. The man who was researching gravitational waves at the university. The man who had been a famous actor until he retired, and his son, also in the entertainment business, who was there too. The woman who had been an executive at the local branch of an interstellar business, until some irregularities regarding client data— she was rather vague on the topic—made her decide it was a good time to retire.

As night fell, Herne asked, "Is there a place to stay around here?"

"Sure," said the bartender. "There are rooms available upstairs." He made a quick motion under the bar, and a minute later a young woman came in. "Missy will help check you in."

"Arrr!" the crowd shouted as Herne stumbled off, and he replied in kind. He followed Missy up the stairs, took the key from her, collapsed into bed, and immediately fell asleep.

Interlude

She heard them first, of course, their stomping and the alarms and the screams. Next came the smell, an overpowering stench of putrescine and other chemicals engineered specifically to trigger a sense of terror in their victims. She had been writing in her journal, a journal probably no one would ever read now, writing and sketching pictures of her younger brother reading in his bunk. This was supposed to have been a "fun" family vacation, like her parents could even imagine what fun was. Fun was back in Jurassia, playing hide and seek with her friends and running laps chasing the little dinosaurs. Fun was not leaving all her friends behind, even the few new friends she had just met since they got here. Fun was not being cooped up in a spaceship—at least for the move, she got to be in suspension the whole time and could pretend it was all a dream. And of course, wasn't it just her luck they'd be attacked by pirates. Her parents probably deserved it, for what they had put her through, but her brother wasn't that bad, most of the time. And she didn't even have a proper boyfriend yet, now she was going to be raped and sold as a slave.

She saw her brother dive into the luggage trunk. He was clever—not as clever as she was, of course, but she had to admit he had some of it. The trunk would have been too small for her anyway, with her lanky legs that didn't seem to want to stop growing. But the closet, she thought that might be a good spot. She dropped her journal and her sweater on top of the trunk, making it look like it hadn't been opened recently so the pirates wouldn't think to look for anyone hiding there, stepped into the closet, and pulled the door closed just as the outer door was smashed apart and one of the pirates walked in. She was too late, though; he had seen the movement on the closet door, grabbed it back open and yanked her out by her arm, nearly dislocating her shoulder. She screamed, but that was only drowned out by the hundreds of other screams in the ship from passengers being similarly abducted.

She gave her captor a kick to the crotch—that's what her parents had taught her—but it was no good with their armored suits on, just caused her to scream again from the pain to her shin. And the pirate leered down at her, with a horny grin as he scanned her still developing chest. Great, now she had given him the idea, and she felt naked despite being fully dressed; she tried to pull her arms across her chest, but he was still holding one of them tight. Luckily, he only paused for a moment, then turned back to dragging her out to the hall.

She heard her parents call out her name from behind her —they must have just seen her. Hopefully they wouldn't be their normal stupid selves and call out her brother's name too. That would be just like them, and she wondered how she and her brother had managed to turn out so well when their parents didn't seem to have one smart gene between them. She smelled smoke and out of the corner of her eye saw some flames down another passageway—someone must have tried to start a fire to hold off the pirates, or maybe the pirates had started it, who knew. It wasn't going to be enough to make a difference in any case.

They took her onto their ship, tiny and cramped compared to the luxury quarters they had been enjoying, with everyone shackled to the walls rather than stretching out in comfortable beds. She couldn't see her parents anywhere now, or hear them, but there were so many sounds—babies crying, parents wailing, screams of pain from those injured, moans from those dying—it was impossible to make out any particular one.

She didn't know what these pirates had in mind for her, but one thing was for sure. If this was the low point in her life, everything crumbling to ashes around her, she was going to find a way to rise back up. And to make sure she remembered this promise to herself, from now on, if anyone asked, her name would be Phoenix.

Chapter 13

It seems we were not headed to Olympia after all. The route we took was extremely round-about. I could only assume we were guided that way on purpose, but the trip was taking three times as long as it would have if we had gone directly from the Dyson sphere entrance. It's not like we needed gravitational assists to save fuel; our fusion engines are running well under capacity. Nor were the passengers awake to enjoy the sights—the outer planet rings, the mountains and valleys of the desert planet, great colorful cloud patterns in swirls and stripes, and active volcanoes, as we passed by nearly every planet in the system. Some of the crew suspect it must have been to avoid detection somehow; others thought it might just be timing, perhaps we were too early and needed to delay a bit. Neither of those really made sense, although without knowing what was going on it was hard to say anything with confidence. Takashi was tempted to ignore one of the directions, just head straight in, but the pirates made it very clear that if he wanted to stay in navigation—which we all understood to mean not be terminated completely—he would follow along with every step as commanded. Finally, right now we are decelerating quickly over Eleusis itself, meaning we completely skipped the Olympia quarantine, which will not make anyone happy if we are seen. That does explain our route, though, since the last time they would have seen us we would have still been pointed toward Olympia, and I'm sure whatever the plan is, we will be in and out of here as fast as possible. I guess if we do it right we could even arrive at Olympia and pass it off as a few close orbits to please the passengers ... who are still asleep, hmmm. But the reality is we are going to land soon. As a low-density asteroid, Eleusis's gravity is fairly weak, low enough that they don't bother with an elevator, so this won't be a problem for us. As long as we don't get caught.

Down below, we can see the Pilgrimage site, the entrance to the underground labyrinth, and the spring that manages to flow despite the low gravity. Even not knowing what it is, it would stand out on what is otherwise a barren surface, pock-marked with craters but showing no signs of native, organic life. But the entrance has a huge wall, with towers acting as beacons, signaling to any passing ships that something is important there. A secondary wall marks the main landing area, separated from the actual entrance by a couple kilome-ters for the safety of the pilgrims and to avoid damage to the labyrinth. It looks like we'll be touching down on the far side, though, away from where most of the pilgrims' ships have landed. As far as I know, nobody has mapped out all the inte-rior passages, but we may be aiming to set down right over top of the center, the location of the Eleusinian Totem itself.

* * *

We have landed on Eleusis. The landing itself was uneventful; as I said, gravity is low enough here that we were able to settle in nicely. That doesn't mean I liked it, though; just because we can doesn't mean it's good for my ship—we usually hang out in orbit and use shuttles to go down to the planet's surface, or occasionally dock directly at a space elevator terminal if it can handle ships of our size. Gravity's bad enough, but atmosphere is the real killer. Even a thin one like there is here—just enough for humans to breathe without spacesuits, but much lower than the typical inhabited areas of most planets—it always seems to result in something getting worn or damaged, and as the head engineer I'm responsible for taking care of that. This time, it looks to be a couple of the airlocks taking on some dust. Not a big deal, just something we—really, I—will need to keep an eye on once we're back out in the vacuum of space. If the pumps get contaminated we'll have a real problem, and the ship won't even launch if it thinks an airlock has failed.

At least nobody at the Pilgrimage entrance seemed to notice us, or if they did they are focused on their own activities and probably figure we're some kind of official vehicle they don't need to concern themselves with. In any case, nobody has tried to walk over to us—we're a bit far for that anyway— or send a scout vehicle to check us out. That's probably good; with the pirates controlling our weapons, I don't think it would end well for anyone too curious.

Now there is a lot of activity going on near the airlock where the pirate ship docked with us. I still have no access to any sensors over there, though, so all I can detect is mass shifting around causing balance changes and vibrations in the rest of the ship's hull. In fact, immediately after the landing, all external sensors were disabled also. I guess they must have brought over some kind of equipment, which is what they were hiding from us, some robotic machinery that they plan to use to infiltrate the caverns. That would raise quite a fuss from the pilgrims, though, if they saw something like that show up in a place that is supposed to be free of any technology.

With even more sensors disabled now, I wonder if the pirates will be stretched too thin, trying to limit us too much that someone will be able to peek through the curtain. I wonder if any of us will be brave enough to try. Not me—as long as we don't try to fly with our sensors off, I'm happy to sit here and rest. Takashi is the one I'm worried about, he's been the most vocal about resistance.

* * *

Well, that's interesting. Even without external sensors, internal vibration detectors are picking up something, and the pattern matches the sound of a drill boring into the rock below us. It's hard to judge based on the echoes—it would be better if I had internal and external to compare—but it sounds like it is at least a meter wide. Which is awfully large to just be sending a robotic probe through, and much larger than I expected the Eleusinian Totem would be. Takashi is curious about this, too; he, Ani, and I have been talking about it, quietly because if the pirates realize we're listening in this way they'll surely disable those sensors too. Are they really trying to extract something that large? And heavy, if it's made of stone that would be several tons—even with the lower gravity here that's a lot of extra mass to lift. Manageable, yes, but expensive, so it would have to be worth a lot. The hole should be big enough to pass a human through, but if they're kidnapping it would be much easier to do at the entrance. None of us had a good answer.

* * *

I guess someone was thinking along the same lines as me about testing the pirates, or just decided he was too uncomfortable not knowing what was going on, with so many sensors disabled, maybe figuring that it would be safer on land than in space. Surprisingly not Takashi, but I would bet that Takashi talked him into it somehow. Whatever he was thinking, one of the remaining communication ems tried to reconfigure a comm antenna as a radar transceiver. Technically that's not a problem, and if he had asked me to help, I might have been able to show him how to do it more subtly. But who knows who can be trusted now—if he had come to me and I had turned him in to the pirates, it would not have gone well for him. I wouldn't have done that, but I probably wouldn't have helped him either; I don't see the point risking my life just to get some low rez images. But the way he did it, they were on to him immediately. We all got a glimpse of the hole—I was right about its size, and I didn't see any large machinery, just a cable I assume is connected to the drill, so I assume if there's anything else out there it's already down below the surface. But the pirates made a clear example of him, proving that they have not softened since the initial boarding. It makes me shudder, or would if I had a body to shudder with, the worst possible ending for an em. They could have just quickly terminated all his processes. But no, they slowly added connection after connection, shorting all his neural centers together, essentially driving him mad. Shunted him to an isolated core, so he wouldn't damage anyone else, then that core was removed from the ship by a robotic arm and left on the surface of Eleusis, with enough solar power to keep running, albeit slowly, for eternity. Yeah, I'm not letting that happen to me. Even Takashi is shaken—he ribs me just as much about surrendering, even seems to blame me for the guy's death, which is crazy because more of them would have died if I hadn't, but he's quieter about it now, more careful that none of his anger is picked up by the pirates. If only I could get him to see it's better to just get along.

Chapter 14

Sybil woke up to a bang on her door. What had happened to her security ems? She should have had plenty of warning. Before she had time to consider what was going on, her door broke down, and two nondescript men dressed in black trench coats and sunglasses ran in. She sat up as quickly as she could, and as she did, one of the men grabbed her hands, making sure to cover her wrist terminal, and yanked them behind her back. The other knocked her glasses onto the floor and crushed them beneath his heel. It was possible they weren't destroyed completely and she could still access them through her jaw implant, but she didn't think it was likely to do her any good, especially if her security ems were already deactivated.

"Ma'am, you'll have to come with us. Now."

"What happened? Who are you?"

"You'll have an opportunity to ask questions later. For now, all I can say is you are coming with us." Cuffs were slapped around her wrists, and she was forced up out of bed.

"Can't I at least get dressed first?" That might get her some access if she could pick out the right outfit. Besides, she would be cold if she were stuck in her nightgown for however long this might take.

"No. You will come as you are."

"What if I was naked?" she shot back, but she could anticipate his response.

"Be glad you're not."

Something was familiar about the second man, the one who had been silent so far, although he was the type of man that she might see every day and never notice. She struggled as best she could, flailing her body from side to side, but they only tightened their grip on her. Together they shoved her through the splintered door and toward a vehicle waiting outside. Her screams brought no help, so as they pushed her into the back seat of the car, she turned and bit down on one of the arms that gripped her shoulder. Unfortunately, that only caused her to emit a cry of intense pain; his sleeve must have been metallized, causing a short in her implant. She could feel the burn marks through her jaw, and tears fell from her eyes unbidden as she sat, no longer able to fight.

Driving through the city at night was beautiful. She normally loved seeing the buildings all lit up and the activity along the main streets, even at this hour, though circumstances prevented her from enjoying it tonight. Here was an acrobat troupe doing a high wire act across the square, there a group of drunks bursting into song as they left the bar, and a passing couple joining in with enthusiasm, but all she could think about was how they could have caught her, and how much they might know. These were obviously not local police, but it could still be just a fishing expedition. On the other hand, if they knew everything … well, in that case, she probably wouldn't be alive to consider the possibilities, too many enemies would have too much motive for revenge. But if they knew just a little, then she was in a tricky position, since denying the obvious evidence would raise their suspicions but, at the same time, giving them any new information would get her in deeper trouble.

The early jobs, little ones, probably meant nothing; they were too far in the past to matter now anyway. As for the files she stole for Infiniti, Greco-Delphi might carry a grudge, maybe even a personal one if one of the execs had taken the blame, but she had covered her tracks well there: several layers of routing indirection on every connection she made, anonymous postings and UBC receiver certificates, and none of the cash had even been spent yet, so there was nothing she could think of that would possibly point to her. The gravity wave setup? She snorted, causing the men to turn briefly and glance at her; that student had been so clueless and the setup so amateur he probably wouldn't have noticed if she had left a big sign saying "pwned", or if he did notice he would have assumed it was an actual alien signal mocking him. The Dyson sphere hack had the same protections as infiltrating Greco-Delphi, although she realized that if she had found one flaw in the protocol, it was possible there were others which would have opened her traffic up for snooping. What would be the odds of two critical flaws, though? Then hiding *Hispaniola*'s tracks as it careened around the system, that was child's play—literally, she had done something similar when she was seventeen just on a bet. But unless this was just a routine kidnapping—which she highly doubted, as they would have told her their ransom goals in that case—she must have missed something somewhere.

"Where are you taking me?" she tried asking, then repeated the question louder when they didn't answer. On the third try, she started kicking the seat in front of her, desperate to get some answer.

"Quiet back there!" Well, at least it was a response, she thought. "We told you, you get to ask no questions until you answer ours."

It wasn't much later when they passed through a gate and into a covered garage, where they parked in front of the only door. As they came around to pull her out of the car, she pulled up her knees and prepared to kick at whoever tried to grab her; it might not stop them, but it would at least make her feel better. Before they opened her door, though, she smelled a sweet gas and her mind started to feel foggy, slow reactions, now the door was open isn't that nice and they're grabbing her ankles and pulling her out and her head hit the ground oh well time to sleep.

* * *

Sybil woke up strapped to a chair in an otherwise empty white-walled room, bright lights glowing through the ceiling. Her mouth felt numb and tasted metallic; she figured they must have removed her implants completely, not relying on the earlier short to have done enough permanent damage. They had even removed her nightgown, replacing it with an even thinner medical-style gown, not smart fabric, and that meant they knew her well, which was not good news for her. At least they had kept the room warm.

When the two men entered, she remembered where she had seen the one before. He looked like the one who had been watching her run on the beach. She wanted to smack herself; all this time being paranoid, thinking she was seeing him everywhere she looked even when he wasn't there, and it had taken her this long to recognize him when he actually was. Blame it on the stress and shock of the arrest, she figured. Although now that she thought about it, it had been over a hundred years ago, and he didn't seem to have aged any more than she had. Maybe he was a descendant, coincidentally the same age? Maybe he had entered a suspension pod, too, somehow synchronized with hers? That would mean they knew a lot, and that he was willing to go to extreme measures to catch her, which would be scary. Maybe whatever organization had taken her had found a way to prevent aging entirely—though given how rich that would make anyone on the open market she didn't really believe that technology could be kept secret; on the other hand maybe it had happened while she was in suspension and she had missed it in her tech review when she woke up. None of the possibilities she considered were really good; however he had managed it, a hundred years was a lot of time to investigate her past, and as good as she thought she was, she had never stayed in one system long enough to consider what might be learned by a very patient codebreaker.

"Now will you tell me why I'm here?"

"Not yet, ma'am. You will answer our questions first. Then we may answer yours. If you are cooperative enough."

She wondered why the man she recognized—or thought she recognized, perhaps she was just being paranoid—wasn't saying anything. Was he just there to observe? As muscle in case she resisted? More to the point, she wondered what kind of hidden comm he might have, and whether there might be some way she could take advantage of it.

"First, we know about the Greco-Delphi job. You thought you were being clever, but the Elsinore data was a plant. When Infiniti started making moves in the market based on it, it was clear the data they were using were sourced to Maryanne Burton. Which turned up the discrepancy in remote access logs—the em you befriended was very helpful to us once he realized what he had done. Anything more you want to tell us about?"

Okay, they knew she had done it. That didn't mean they knew how. If they didn't, there was still hope, since they couldn't follow leads based on her technology.

"Yes, well, corporate espionage is a big thing, you know. So who are you, and why isn't Greco-Delphi taking care of me themselves?"

"We're not done with our questions. Again, is there anything else you want to tell us?"

"I suppose you know about my quantum cryptor."

"We know you have one. Our team's analyzing it right now to learn its capabilities and figure out where you got it from. But that's not what I'm asking. Are there any other jobs?"

This was where she had to walk a fine line. She couldn't just say no; they would never believe that Greco-Delphi had been her first, as that was something she would have had to work up to. "Yes. Before I came to the system, I—"

"No," he interrupted. "Here. Now. What job are you working on?"

"What do you mean?"

"See, that's not being cooperative. So, no, we won't answer your questions. And if you don't change your mind, we can do drugs, we can do shock, we can do electroneural scanner implants. There's all kinds of things we can do."

"Phoenix." She had heard tales of the implants, technology similar to what was used to create brain emulations, but coarser and cheaper. Minds could be destroyed that way, after they were read out fully. Or so the stories went, always a friend of a friend who had suffered through it, nobody willing to admit that they had succumbed themselves or able to explain how they knew so much about what happened to the alleged victim, so who knew how much they might be exaggerated. Needless to say, she knew it was highly illegal, in this or any civilized system, so it would be used only by someone who was above the law, authorized or at least shielded at the highest levels.

"Huh?"

"That's the client's name: Phoenix."

"Who is he?"

"I don't know anything else about him ... or her, I don't even know that much. I have signed UBC blockchains—you can have them if you want—but I tried to trace them back to a person and couldn't. All completely anonymized transactions, routed through fake exchanges, but the certs all line up and everyone agrees they're legit. Go ahead and try yourselves, maybe get back to me in another hundred years after you've failed too. All I know is I was hired to do a job and I got paid when it was done."

"What's the job?"

"I don't know the details. Something on Eleusis. I just guided the ship there, I'm not involved in the acquisition."

"When does it get to Eleusis? Traces haven't seen any ship heading that way."

Sybil smiled at that. She had done her job well. "It landed yesterday, followed camouflaged routes and stayed shielded from sensors, then landed fast."

"Shit! Alright, you'll stay here until we have him. You want out sooner, you start telling us more."

"I would if I could, but really, that's all I know."

The men walked out and left her there.

Before they closed the door, she called out, "Hey! You still haven't told me who you are!"

The second man, the one who had been silent so far, ducked his head back in and said, "Sorry, not happening." Then he slammed the door, and she was left alone again.

Chapter 15

Herne woke up groggy and hungover. Luckily he would have a few days in the space elevator to clear his head before getting back on his ship. After a shower, he headed down to breakfast, unsurprised to see many of the same people still there, or maybe back already. This was a way of life for some, he knew, and while Herne could enjoy it once in a while, he was careful not to let it stop him from having other adventures. He greeted some of his new-found friends but ate his breakfast quietly in the corner rather than joining them. It was time to start on the quiet contemplation, the preparation for the Pilgrimage. He thought back on his life so far, the good—most of the last thirty years on Jurassia—the bad—the way he left his family—and the ugly—well, he wasn't ready to contemplate all of that yet, some of the things he had gotten mixed up in before he settled in Jurassia, the people he shouldn't have befriended, the things he did for them. The time would come when he would have to face those, the rituals of the Pilgrimage would demand it, but not now, not with a hangover. As he finished his meal he gave a quick wave goodbye, hardly even noticed by the regulars who had settled back into their routine and he made his way back to the space elevator.

The city looked different this morning, quieter than the night before, with not nearly as much movement. That would come later, but for now, Herne could walk slowly without worrying about getting knocked off the walkway. It felt more like a quiet walk in the wilds of Jurassia; sure, there were tall skyscrapers in place of trees, an occasional pocket of people outside a restaurant instead of a herd of dinosaurs congregating around a watering hole. Despite all the time he had spent away from cities, he could quickly feel at home here, at least at this time of day. And the streets formed a sort of labyrinth of their own, making him think of the Pilgrimage that he would start soon. He saw a cat dart across the street, a flash of fur that he could barely make out the gray color on; looking up he saw he was walking past a church—not Nupist, and the cat probably wasn't living there, but still he smiled as it reminded him of the temple cats he would be seeing soon.

The start of his trip back up the elevator was uneventful, but about a quarter of the way up, an urgent override came through on the compartment's terminal.

"Herne Sutherland?"

"Yes…?" Usually these overrides were broadcast messages, to announce delays, warnings of high meteor activity, or the like, but he had never seen one directed to him, or anyone, personally.

"My name is Carol Petrova. I'm captain of security here on Olympia. I understand you're a hunter."

"Thirty years on Jurassia, best hunt guide on the planet if I do say so myself."

"And I understand you know something about pirates."

Herne snorted. "Sure, Magellan gave me something about authorizing pirate hunting or something like that. I suppose you got the message, too. Nothing came of it, though."

"Well, we have a problem. We have received information that pirates are raiding Eleusis, probably as we speak."

"Eleusis? No shit! That's where I was heading!"

"How's your ship? Fast?"

"Oh yeah, should be able to get there in a day, once I get to the top here."

"We have a shuttle waiting for you at the next maintenance point. You should be there in ten minutes. Please get off the elevator and take it directly to your ship." If Herne had had any doubt before, this was enough to make the urgency clear. Using shuttles from anywhere below the end of an elevator was almost unheard of, an extravagance saved only for when time absolutely could not be wasted.

"Do you know what the pirate is after? A raid on Eleusis … lots of pilgrims there I suppose, is that it?"

"We don't know yet, but two of my men are working on trying to figure that out. But given what we do know, about the efforts they took to get into the system, this doesn't seem like just a slaving run. There are easier ways to do that than coming so close in."

"But why do you need me? Don't you have your own system security forces that could take care of him?"

"We do, but unfortunately, we can't be sure they're not compromised. There was a lot of effort behind this, and we've already seen some evidence of security ships being reprogrammed, navigation systems failing if trying to plot a course toward the pirate ship, fusion drives shutting down entirely near Eleusis. We have captured one spy that was working for the pirates here on Olympia, but until we know the full extent of the hack and can undo everything, we can only trust ships from out of system. So it's lucky you came along when you did. At least, I'm hoping yours is still unaffected."

"Alright, so what do you want me to do?"

"Get to your ship. Chase the pirates down. Kill them. The leader's name is Phoenix, by the way, if that means anything to you."

"No, never heard it before."

"Okay. Wait—I just got a report that an unidentified ship was spotted on Eleusis, at some distance from the main entrance, just taking off when the message was sent. That must be the pirates. Contact me directly if there's anything I can do to help, and if we learn more, I will let you know. We'll send you what we know about the pirate ship—type, appearance, last known location—once you're on your ship."

With that, Carol's face disappeared from the screen. Herne thought for a moment. As much as he hated interrupting his Pilgrimage, if the pirate was raiding Eleusis then the Pilgrimage wasn't much of an option anyway. And a hunt ... well, this would be quite a bit different than hunting animals. More dangerous for him, certainly, but danger was always part of the thrill, one reason why he never resorted to guns against dinosaurs because just having that as a backup would eliminate the risk. Most of all, he felt something of a duty, if there was anything he could do to help defend the holy site.

When the elevator stopped at the access point—because this was so unusual it led to all kinds of questioning faces among the other passengers, not to mention cursing from those who feared a significant delay—Herne got off and worked his way through the maintenance tunnels to where the shuttle was docked. This would get him to his ship in minutes instead of the days that would have remained on the elevator, albeit at a much greater cost in energy, but clearly time was critical here. If the pirate got away from Eleusis, there would be plenty of places to hide in this system, to gain time to plot an escape through the Dyson sphere, so Herne wanted to do everything possible to stop him before that happened. Once aboard his ship, he checked out weapons systems (fully operational) and engines (same), and he programmed navigation for the fastest route to Eleusis. The hunt was on!

But with that, the memories started coming back. The mobsters sending him a name, maybe a location but if not then it was his job to find them. Hunt them down. Make sure they would never cheat his bosses again, or threaten their business, or disrespect them, or whatever little thing they had done to get on his list, because for some of his bosses it didn't take much. How many planets had he done that on? Three, four? How many close calls had there been, when he found himself on the opposing mob's list, in a race to see which assassin would hit his mark first, and which would never get a job again? Now, thinking back, how many close calls might there have been that he didn't even know about? He knew from his side how a coincidence of timing—a missed train, or a crowd of people passing down the street—could be enough to throw off his plans. It was so much better hunting dinosaurs; as fierce and dangerous as they were, at least he didn't have to worry about a bullet coming toward him if he stepped around the wrong corner. So now he was back in this game, man against man. But he needed to put his past behind him, focus on his duty, and get this job done. For the Pilgrimage.

Chapter 16

Still waiting. The sound of drilling continues, but that's all I know. It reminds me of my early jobs on the drilling rigs on Earth, before fusion technology was advanced enough to replace oil everywhere. I certainly had to put up with more than my share of harassment for that job ("Fish killer! Don't you know you're cooking the world! Get with the future!") despite the fact that oil was still critical for some transportation systems that everyone relied on, and I was just doing my job trying to support that need. It's not like I didn't know that was going to be a short-lived job; everyone knew fusion was getting cheaper and oil was getting more expensive as it got rarer and harder to drill. It was actually a relief for me when it finally shut down and I started my new career in the space program, doing my best to hide my job history from anyone who might think less of me because of it. One thing I did learn, though, is the sound of a drill. I could tell the speed of the drill, the type of rock, even what was coming up ahead based on echoes. I'm not sure what good it does me now, but at least I know we're drilling outside.

The destruction of the communication em has had a chilling effect on the rest of us. Even normal conversation is limited to what is absolutely necessary for operation of the ship, nobody wanting to take the risk of something being overheard and misinterpreted as some kind of coded message. An innocent question like "what is the status of life support?" results in an abrupt "I don't know. Go check yourself!" Probably an overreaction, but if that was the goal of the pirates with their merciless torture, they certainly succeeded. Even Takashi sounds more subdued lately, although it hasn't stopped him from dropping subtle hints that maybe some sabotage while we're on the ground would be helpful to the cause. What cause exactly? Even here on Eleusis, we're still under the thumb of the pirates.

I wonder how much longer before our stay starts to attract attention? Someone in the center of the labyrinth would normally take two to three days to work their way out; but if they sensed something wrong they could probably make it out in a day. Would they notice the drilling? Hard to say, maybe not if they are fully focused on their ritual. But at some point, the drill will break through, and if we actually take something, yeah, it will be noticed then. And I assume the plan is to take something; if the goal was just destruction, then a hydrogen bomb would be more effective. Hopefully, we'll be able to make a quick exit when that time comes.

* * *

After two days of drilling, the vibration stopped, and shortly afterward, external sensors were turned back on. Sure enough, there is a big hole in the ground, but no evidence of what passed through it, and still no sign of any mechanical arms, so they must have retracted those already. It's got to be something big, though. Maybe when we take off I'll be able to estimate how much mass we've gained, although if the pirates really wanted to hide that, they could easily have dumped fuel to balance it out. I guess we'll see. Also, as I expected, we are not going to be left alone long. We are over the horizon from the start of the Pilgrimage, so nobody can see us directly, but we are picking up radio chatter, and it's clear that people by the entrance are concerned about something. They'll be sending scouts out soon; if they don't know our exact direction it may take hours, maybe even a day, but we don't have much time, and if there are any ships parked in stationary orbit they'll be able to pinpoint us more quickly. I hear our weapons being prepared just in case, and directions from Phoenix are to prepare to leave Eleusis immediately. I don't know how we plan to exit the system. Will we have help like before? Or is there some other plan? One problem at a time.

* * *

That was close. Of course, the one time that it is critical that you leave quickly is when you run into trouble. We were trying to take off, but there was a problem with the airlock, the one the pirate ems are still guarding jealously. Even though the area was (and still is) sealed off, the ship knew it was there and wouldn't start up the engines without knowing it was sealed.

It's a standard safety measure; it's one thing when you're already in space and you have to continue one way or another, but a failed dock is something you would absolutely want to fix before leaving safe ground. As ship engineer, it was up to me to "fix" it, even though nothing was broken. (Or maybe it is broken? There's no way for me to know.) And Phoenix made it very clear what would happen to me, and all the engineering crew, if we couldn't.

"Can't we just enable the sensors around the dock?" I tried asking. "That would take care of it."

"No! You're the brilliant engineer. Find a way around it. Or you can join your friend out there on the surface. If someone doesn't come by and bomb us before I can kill you myself."

We tried the simple solutions, first routing duplicate data from another airlock to the invisible one, but that just raised alarms on the other airlock. Any other sensor was insufficient, also, since the data didn't match. It didn't help that Phoenix and the other pirate ems were constantly checking on us, asking when we would able to take off. I also heard from the monitors that probes had been sent out from the entrance, luckily not directly toward us yet, but their scan pattern would bring them into view soon. If I had been human, I would have been sweating, adrenaline rushing through my body, sharpening my senses and helping my brain make connections. As an em, I was sped up, brain working four times as a fast a standard human brain, signals rushing in and communication messages whisking back and forth between us. It's a rush, living at that speed; most of us can't handle it for long.

In the end, Ani came up with the plan that worked. We did have a small printer on board, in case human passengers needed anything during a voyage, though I couldn't remember the last time it had been used. With that, we were able to print a new set of airlock control systems. It took some work to patch them into the comm network—all the communications ems needed to be assigned to help us get it done quickly—but once they were, they could be routed to override the airlock behind the pirate blackout. That gave us the right number of "functioning" airlocks, according to the safety checks, and launch releases were cleared. Everything seems to be working now, so we have started up the fusion drive and will be on our way up off this asteroid any time now. Which is good, because a probe just briefly appeared over the horizon and then turned back. Maybe it missed us and is still scouting, but we have to assume it saw us and is reporting back our position, which means weaponry will follow soon. We can't be off this asteroid soon enough if you ask me.

Chapter 17

Sybil waited. And waited. Waiting was boring. She knew she had to do something. Whoever it was that had her, they were clearly some high up government agency or similar organization, and just as clearly they were not going to let her go. If they managed to stop Phoenix, they would probably kill her. If they weren't able to stop Phoenix, they would probably torture her to try to get more information that she didn't have, or maybe just kill her out of spite. If they were actually working for Phoenix and this was some kind of a test, they probably would have killed her already, so at least she could rule that out. But if they didn't kill her, and Phoenix didn't get caught—or if Phoenix had other partners that could track her down later—she'd probably be in just as much trouble for not having kept quiet. So she had to escape and somehow warn Phoenix, in order to redeem herself. But how to escape?

She assessed her situation: strapped to a chair, wearing only a natural fiber gown, oral implants offline, in a room with a single door, who knows where in the building, and she had to assume there were cameras watching her and probably gas that could be piped in if she tried anything. So her greatest talent, computer hacking, was no use right now. As for feminine wiles, the two guys she had met had shown no interest in that, and she didn't know how long it would be before they would even show up again. That meant she was going to have to force her way out, with some mixture of athleticism and cleverness that she hoped would result in success, even as she didn't really know exactly how.

The first step would be getting unstrapped. The strap went around her waist and pinned her arms behind the chair; at least her wrists weren't tied together anymore. She sucked in her gut as tight as she could to give her arms as much space as possible, then popped her right shoulder up hard, out of its socket. "Ow! Fuck!" she screamed, but it worked; her right hand was loose. Wincing from the pain, she was able to push the strap low enough to get her left hand out, then try to set her shoulder back in place. She was used to running through pain, but this was a different level; still, she kept her mind focused on what needed to be done. Her ankles were tied separately to the chair, but she was able to stand up, hop over to the wall, and with a spinning kick smash it against the wall, breaking it—and her ankle in the process—but at least she could move freely now, albeit with a limp.

This time, she heard the gas before she smelled it. Thinking fast, she took off the gown, forgoing modesty in favor of survival, and formed a bubble of air pulled tight against her mouth and nose. That might give her a minute or two at best before she ran out of oxygen, but she was determined to make

the most of it. At least she knew that nobody would be entering the room until the gas was dispersed, so she didn't have to
worry about that; once she was out, it would be a different
story, though.

The door was, as she expected, electronically controlled.
And she had long ago figured out how to handle that, with
everything she needed implanted in her thumb; it only worked
at very short range, which meant it had been no use earlier, but
which also had prevented them from finding it and deactivat-
ing it, probably by cutting off her thumb. She took one last
deep breath, bundled up her gown in one hand and grabbed
the chair in the other as a shield, then put her thumb up
against the door. After what seemed like forever to her but was
only two seconds, she heard a giant fan spin up, sucking the
remains of the gas out of the room, and then the door latch
released. Certainly, anyone in the hall would be watching her,
ruining any possible element of surprise, but this was the best
she could do. She pushed the door open and threw her gown
out, hoping at least to force a few seconds of blindness on her
captors, and holding her chair in front of her chest, she ran out
of the room. After just one step, though, the run turned into a
hobble as her broken ankle reminded her of its condition, and
she gave up, waiting for the inevitable bullet. But after a few
seconds, when the bullet hadn't come, she looked around, and
finally realized the hall was empty.

They had to know she was up to something. They wouldn't
have released the gas otherwise, since they would want her to
be lucid for interrogation if necessary, so someone must have

been watching. Maybe just an em, though, if all the humans were otherwise occupied. She hadn't been gone long enough for her fail-safe to have started, had she? That was a good question; she realized she didn't know exactly how long she had been out from the gas, so maybe it had, maybe that was keeping everyone busy trying to work around the havoc it would have started. Or maybe this was a trap, luring her some-where; why they'd bother she had no idea, but she'd have to be careful until she was out of here. Which raised another good question; she still didn't know where "here" was.

She put her gown back on and stumbled down the hall until she found an open room with a terminal inside. Her first priority would be to hide the evidence; even if it was only ems watching, they would be setting off alarms and would know which room she was in now, and it wouldn't be long before someone was there and drugged her again, or just shot her. She tried to access the security camera system through the ter-minal, but she was denied.

"You must remain where you are," the security em spoke up. "Someone will be there shortly to return you to your cell."

"Listen, fucker. I'm desperate. And I will terminate you if I need to. Now let me through."

"Sorry, I can't do that. You are a prisoner here."

Why was this em even talking to her? This was definitely a government agency. For all the apparent viciousness of her first encounter, the limitations of bureaucracy were evident, and she could take advantage of that. "Well, at least can you tell me where I am?"

"Olympia System Security Underground Holding Cell." Well, that was something—underground meant she needed to go up, and System Security meant standard government routines, which should mean no surprises. Now, if she could just mess with this em a bit.

"And since I'm stuck here, what's your name?"

"You can call me Guy."

"Are you the one who released the gas in my holding cell, Guy?"

"Yes, that was me. Clever idea with the gown. I didn't think to disable the door, though; they should have done a more thorough check for implants."

"Yeah, well, I'm sure they'll find a way to blame that on you, too. How long have you been a guard here?"

"Subjective or objective time? I guess you'd say 40 years."

"Wow, and you still haven't figured out how to watch your own back." While she had been distracting the em with conversation, she had been quickly doing a memory scan on the terminal, then modifying a running script to transform it into a virus that would destroy the first em that it encountered. A first-rate security em would have noticed her and stopped her before she got anywhere. Then again, a first-rate em wouldn't be stuck working down here.

"What?" Guy asked, which was enough for the virus to lock onto his quantum processing logic and interrupt the connections, effectively killing him. Now Sybil was free to access the security records. She quickly deleted the video from the hallway, the part showing her entering this room and several minutes beyond that, hoping it would lead anyone to think she had gone much further. That would only help fool late-arriving reinforcements—if any humans had already seen where she'd gone, she couldn't overwrite their memories—but it was the best she could do. She created a log entry saying that she had already been recaptured; again, that wouldn't stop someone from hunting her down, but at least it might cause fewer people to take an interest in her, and anything that would make her escape easier was worth trying.

She retraced her steps past her cell, still limping from the broken ankle, until she found a stairwell. Listening for the sound of footsteps, she heard nothing, so she went inside and started climbing up. The door she had gone through was marked "SB2"; three flights of stairs should get her to the ground floor. Just before she got to the main basement floor, the door flew open and two men entered, the same two that had captured her originally, which made her think there must be a very small staff here. They were shocked to see her in front of them, and she took advantage of the surprise. She grabbed the railing and kicked up with her good leg to knock over the silent one, just as he was drawing his gun. She then pushed off the railing, grabbed the gun as it slipped from his hand, landed—not entirely on her good foot, and the pain shot up her leg, but she had to ignore it for now—and quickly turned and shot the other man. Her first time shooting a gun, it wasn't a great shot, hitting him in the shoulder, but at least it would slow him down a bit. She fired another shot at the man she had fallen on top of, blood spurting from his head and spraying over her gown and face, then aimed back at the other. The first shot caused him to grab his testicles and the second, square in the chest, caused him to fall over dead. She stopped to catch her breath and winced from her throbbing ankle, but she knew she didn't have time to stay here long.

Keeping the gun, thinking it might come in handy again later, Sybil continued up the stairs and found an exit to ground. How happy she was to see open air again! Even though she had often holed up in her own apartment for much longer than she had been trapped in the cell, there was something about being free to leave anytime she wanted that made a huge difference. About a hundred yards away from the building was a small shuttle, apparently unguarded, enough to get her off the planet and hopefully let her rendezvous with Phoenix. If nothing else, she would need to send a warning, and she desperately hoped there would be medical supplies there as well to deal with her ankle. At this point, she was barely able to hop anymore, but she did the best she could, crying out with every other step, and she made it to the shuttle just as more men started exiting the building, firing in her direction.

Luckily for her, the shuttle was open; she could only imagine that it must have recently landed and not been locked up yet. Onboard, she fired up the communication system and sent a broadcast message at full power—anyone else in the system would pick it up as well as Phoenix, but that didn't really matter now. "Be aware: operation compromised. They are after you." She programmed the navigation system toward Eleusis, then remembered her fail-safe and silently cursed her own efficiency. "Navigation: recognize my voice and apply override code 395-1402." Hopefully that part works too, she thought, and she hoped it wasn't her imagination when she felt the shuttle lift off the ground as she finally, mercifully, passed out from the pain.

Chapter 18

Herne was speeding toward Eleusis. Not knowing how he would find the pirate ship—still on the ground, in orbit, or already headed elsewhere—he was maintaining a high velocity as long as he could, at least until he absolutely had to slow down to enter orbit at Eleusis, if that was necessary. He would rather not fall too far behind if it came to a chase; on the other hand, the information he had was that Phoenix's ship was an interstellar information cargo ship, designed to efficiently cruise between systems, not for rapid acceleration, so Herne would have a great advantage if it did come to that. More worrisome, according to the information from New Jupiter, there were five human passengers on board when it left. They apparently checked in when passing through the Dyson sphere, but that might just as well have been some trickery. Regardless, it was unknown whether they were still alive, so Herne had to be careful; just blowing up the ship entirely would need to be a last resort.

A communication request opened up from Eleusis. "Pirate Hunter Herne."

"Yes, we are approaching Eleusis."

"We have confirmed the pirate ship has just launched from Eleusis. Also, we have determined the pirate's quarry. The Eleusinian Totem is missing."

Herne was shocked for a moment. Even though it was not too surprising—the key artifact at the heart of the Pilgrimage was always a likely target—it still hit him hard to hear that it was actually missing. That gave him one more reason to be careful when engaging the pirate. If he obliterated the passengers, he could always tell himself they were probably dead already. But if he destroyed the Eleusinian Totem, such an important icon of his faith, he would never be able to forgive himself.

"Also, you should be aware the Totem is not simply an artifact. It is a breeding ground for an alien lifeform. We don't know how this might affect the situation, but you should know in case it matters."

This far surpassed his original shock, since he would never have imagined it.

"What kind of alien life are we talking about here."

"Microscopic. It's not fully understood yet, not DNA-based so we don't even know how to analyze a genome, but it's a parasite of some form. Or maybe not parasite, maybe symbiote is a better word. It is known to enter the human brain and affect mental operation but doesn't seem to harm the affected person."

"So all those people who appear to have changed personalities after the Pilgrimage...?"

"We don't know really. Some of them certainly, it's caused by the alien. Others could be a true religious experience. As you can imagine, we don't go asking every Pilgrim to submit to a full brain scan afterward."

"Okay, well, I can understand why you'd want to keep that secret. I guess I'm impressed you've been able to actually keep it for so long."

"Well, the theory is out there, but there are so many theories being argued about by people who aren't content accepting the mysteries of Nupism, some of which we've spread intentionally, so it hasn't ever become widely accepted. I hope we can trust you with the truth."

"I swear on all the gods, nobody will know this from my mouth, my hand, my mind."

"Good luck, Pirate Hunter. May Athena guide you." And they signed off.

Well, that was something interesting to know, Herne thought, and it would make it worth taking some extra precautions if he managed to retrieve the Totem. Even though millions of pilgrims had experienced it as part of the Pilgrimage, he didn't know how it would react outside of its normal environment. If the lifeforms were really intelligent in some way, they might not be happy about it. Or worse, the pilgrimage site might have been restraining them somehow, and now they would finally have the chance to work their own will in a way that might not be fully compatible with human survival. No, not likely, Herne laughed. That was science fiction thinking.

While he was thinking about this, Herne's ship detected

the pirate ship, still at some distance, but on a straight trajectory for Herne to intercept. Good, that would make it easier, he thought, and he brought up his navigation em.

"That's the ship we are hunting. Full speed to intercept, do your best to detect and follow any course changes it makes. Allow for up to four gees acceleration."

"On it, sir," the em responded, and Herne felt a sudden jerk as the ship changed direction toward where the pirate was heading.

With navigation under control, Herne focused his own thoughts on strategy. This would have been much easier if he could have trapped the pirate on Eleusis. Ground battles had been fought for millennia before space travel was even imagined, and techniques would be little different than hunting dinos on Jurassia, but with more guns ... and more guns aimed back at him. Space battles, on the other hand, were rare. The vastness of space, the challenge of calculating trajectories and accounting for recoil, the robustness of ships that needed to survive for centuries under bombardment by cosmic rays and micrometeors all conspired to make it difficult to engage and easy to escape. Unless you managed to dock and board, that is, in which case it became a ground battle again, only one with possibly varying gravity, making traditional urban fighting tactics look like a children's game. Boarding was easier said than done; still, he knew it was probably his only real choice.

As he drew closer, Herne decided it was time to engage. He activated one hydrogen bomb and launched it in front of the pirate's path. Especially at this distance, they would see it and evade it with no problem, so he didn't expect a hit; this was just to get their attention. When he saw the explosion, predictably far from the actual pirate ship, he lit up a broadcast communication channel.

"Attention Pirate Phoenix on the Starship *Hispaniola*! This is Pirate Hunter Herne. I am authorized to track you down and destroy you. Please adjust course to set down on the nearest asteroid."

The response came quickly, a female voice received as soon as the light speed round trip delay had passed.

"Greetings 'Pirate Hunter'. Short answer is no. Be aware five human passengers on board are still alive. If you don't stop following me and get me safe passage out through the Dyson sphere that will not be the case for long."

That was more or less the response Herne expected. For all the trouble the pirate had gone through she was never likely to just set down and surrender. But Herne could put some leverage on the side of the hostages, too.

"Sorry, I am not authorized to negotiate, just to stop you. If the passengers are dead, there is nothing to stop me from a full assault, which that mail ship of yours will lose. Even killing one would only convince me of your bloodthirstiness, and I'll act as if they'll all be dead soon anyway. So I suggest you keep them all alive. Once again, I ask you to surrender, and I can promise that you will not be harmed and that you will see a fair trial."

Again, Herne got exactly the response he expected—silence, and the pirate ship accelerating directly away from him as fast as it was capable of going. So that was how the game was going to go—chase, board, win. Herne sometimes did enjoy a high-speed chase, the wind blowing through his hair, the sound of dino feet stomping on the ground echoing across the plain, the blur of the trees rushing by. He would have none of that here, of course. No wind, no sound, not much to see, just the occasional chunk of rock but always far enough away that they would appear to be moving slowly. Yes, he thought, space chases were pretty boring.

"Weapons, keep firing H-bombs around them, keep them going straight."

"Yes, sir."

His fusion drive was running at maximum capacity, and he would catch them before too long. Keeping them going straight would make it easier on him, with fewer jerks from surprise accelerations if his navigation team had to match the pirate's movements. He considered the other weapons he had on hand: neutron bombs, no, that would take out the passengers as well as the pirate, assuming they hadn't been killed already, and he had to assume that they hadn't, since he didn't want to be guilty of killing them. EMPs were too dangerous to his own ship, a last resort if he needed them, but he couldn't rely on his shielding blocking a pulse. Beam guns were more useful as repellers or for cutting through meteors about to cross your path; they'd do nothing against a heavily shielded interstellar vessel. If only he had some kind of rope, a lasso of sorts, he wished, but really, even if it was made of smart nanobots that would curl the way he wanted, he knew there was still no way to make it long enough and keep it strong enough to pull in a ship moving at a tenth the speed of light without ripping it apart. Well, he had plenty of time to ponder and think of alternatives, until he would finally catch up and be able to board. Maybe he wouldn't have to actually board, just dock and tow the ship somewhere, if his own ship had enough thrust to overpower the pirate ship. The pirate would probably force a boarding one way or another, but Herne would be prepared for anything.

He left the control room in the hands of the crew ems and headed to the workout room. That was one of the nice features of this ship. All his previous travels had been in suspension, and if he was woken up a few days before arrival he would be bored out of his mind, crammed in a tiny compartment, not even really able to interact with the other passengers much. This ship was designed for a working human crew, one that would have to stay active and alert, so it had the facilities to support that, even if Herne was the only human on board at this time. It couldn't match being out on a planet, especially a wild one like Jurassia—hiking, climbing, hauling gear, fighting dinosaurs—but any kind of exercise would help keep both his body and mind in good shape. Plus, the walls could simulate the environment of any known planet, so he could at least pretend that he was back at home.

While he was engaged in his workout, racing a pack of virtual troodons through a projected grassy savannah with an erupting volcano in the distance (thankfully without real ash to affect his breathing), his defense ems notified him that they had deflected an incoming bomb. "So, they're shooting back," he thought. At least that would keep the chase a little interesting, although he knew that if he had been in any real danger, he would have been told about the bomb before it was deflected. No question about it, a mail ship would be no match for a warship.

Chapter 19

If my first battle, when Phoenix showed up and took over the *Hispaniola*, came as a complete surprise, the second one was just a matter of time. We got off Eleusis without seeing more than the scouts, but as we left, I could see them reporting back, so we didn't have time to spare. Nobody followed us, though—people on the Pilgrimage aren't really the follow-pirates sort—but we knew if trouble came, it would more likely come from Olympia anyway. Once we got the message from Sybil that her precautions had failed and she had been captured—no matter how hard they tried, the pirates couldn't keep the contents of that message secret from the crew—all of us knew that some-one would be coming for us soon. That put us all on high alert, keeping a close watch on any ships launching from that direc-tion. And when our sensors picked up the first bomb heading toward us, navigation was able to do a slight course correction and give it a wide berth. Of course, it was obviously a warning shot, either that or horribly misaimed, and it wouldn't have hit us even if we had continued on straight ahead, but there's no sense in taking chances, not when the consequences of failure are massive destruction. Even Takashi doesn't try to argue with that logic.

Phoenix has apparently given up trying to limit access to received communications, because we all heard the messages from Herne, too. "Pirate Hunter Herne," that is. (Who gave him that title anyway? Does he really think it makes him sound more important?) I'm sure Phoenix has more important things to think about now, like escaping. Besides, we are all in this together now; if Herne destroys the ship, the entire crew is gone as well, so we have every incentive to get away. So my team's job is to keep the ship going at maximum speed. Navigation looks for any gravity boosts that can help us keep our distance, plus keep us away from any bombs. Communication, well, they're not too busy now; we're still receiving messages from the pirate hunter, but Phoenix doesn't seem interested at all in responding.

Herne clearly has a faster ship than us, one more suited for in-system navigation. We quickly gave up on diversion tactics and went straight for maximum acceleration away from him, but he is still closing in. Hopefully consideration of the passengers will limit the aggressiveness of his attacks, and hopefully Phoenix won't do something stupid like actually start to kill them; Herne made it clear that would have bad consequences. Occasionally a bomb is launched toward us, but none has actually made an impact yet; our evasions and pressure shields have kept them far enough away. As ship engineer, that makes me happy because there's nothing I have to worry about repairing. We return fire, of course, just as a matter of principle, but there's not really much point; if anything he's better defended than we are, and probably more heavily armed, so we'll run out of ammunition long before he does.

It does seem that Herne's is the only ship chasing us, which is surprising. I consider us lucky there, but it's not too much consolation since we are still trapped within the Dyson sphere. Once he has us pinned there, I don't know what our plan could be. Probably Phoenix doesn't know either; I'm sure Sybil was supposed to get us out just as she got us in, or maybe the plan was just to run around inside the sphere until everyone had long forgotten about us—which could take a very long time, especially when you consider augmented human memory and em lifetimes. Well, there is time to figure that one out, or, more likely given current trajectories, it won't matter since Herne will catch up to us first. But until then, this is looking to be more of an extended chase than a proper battle, lots of empty space around us and at least several days, maybe weeks, before he gets close enough to really engage.

* * *

Perhaps luck favors the pirates after all! Today we received another transmission from Sybil. She made it onto a shuttle and off of Olympia. That's a short-range vehicle, so we'll need to adjust course to pick her up before she runs out of life support capacity. Honestly, I'm surprised we're doing that, putting ourselves at more risk rather than just getting as far away as possible and leaving her on her own. But Phoenix was very clear—as soon as the message came through, we got orders to set an intercept course. Hopefully, Herne won't realize who's in the shuttle until we're able to block his line of fire; one of his hydrogen bombs would take out the shuttle without trouble. Our course change will allow him to catch us much sooner, but that was bound to happen anyway, so we may as well get it over with. And Sybil got us this far, so perhaps she can be of some help in the fight.

Takashi disagrees, of course. He figures anyone who is helping a pirate doesn't deserve to be rescued, certainly not at the risk of his own life. Not that he can just ignore the order; that would quickly result in his termination and someone else taking over his role in navigation. But he's got some choices— he can carefully shield the shuttle or leave it exposed, line up for an easy docking or make her do all the work. He's going to have to be careful; if Phoenix detects any funny business he'll be in trouble. I don't understand why he's always so busy coming up with schemes that have no chance of working rather than just going along. I mean, I don't like going along with pirates any more than he does, but that's where we are now, and if we can just get through it, I'm sure we'll be released once we are out of the Olympia system and the pirate ems can transfer back to their ship.

* * *

Well, that was a surprise. The docking maneuvers went smoothly, Takashi made it easy for her after all. But after Sybil entered the airlock, the ems stopped blocking sensors....

Chapter 20

When Sybil finally came to, she looked around at her surroundings. Still in the shuttle, still on course to meet up with Phoenix, still in a shitload of pain. She crawled over to the medical supply cabinet and dug out a syringe filled with painkiller, then stabbed it into her arm. She hoped it would work quickly. She also found a bandage and wrapped her ankle. She'd be lucky if she could run at all after this; really given her situation, she'd be lucky if she even survived, so if she did, perhaps the surgery she'd have to go through would be no more than a minor inconvenience. In the closet by the medical supplies, she also found a uniform of sorts: it was a bit baggy, but better than the prisoner's gown that she was still wearing. She felt much more comfortable after changing into it, more like a human being in control of her own destiny again. It even had a holster for her to keep her gun, though she hoped she wouldn't need to use it again.

Starting to feel better—pain reduced to a bad headache—she looked around for materials she could use to rig up a crutch and keep her from hurting her ankle even more. This was harder than she thought it would be, but then people didn't typically carry pieces of wood around on their spaceships. Duct tape was easy to find in the supply cabinet, though, and eventually she was able to break the plastic arms off a chair in the control room, which was far from perfect but better than nothing. Now able to walk without damaging her ankle further, she went back to the communications terminal. This time, she went through the steps to set up a secure channel to Phoenix and request a rendezvous, knowing that her shuttle didn't have nearly the range to catch up to the ship that seemed to be accelerating at full speed away from her. She wasn't sure if they would come back for her; if her first message had been received, immediate escape may be more of a priority for the pirates, but she hoped that if nothing else, her help may still be needed to get back out through the Dyson sphere. She waited for a response, growing impatient—was she going to be left behind after all? Was the pirates' communication system damaged, preventing them from responding, or maybe even from receiving her message in the first place? It was hard to tell at first, given the speed it was going, whether the ship was maintaining its course. Finally, she breathed a sigh of relief as she saw that the pirate ship was, in fact, changing course toward her, then she nearly lost her breath when she saw the explosion just missing it. This was going to be close; she would have to avoid being detected by the pursuer and meet up with the pirate ship before it was destroyed. Even then, she wondered how long the ship would last with her on it. But she would have to worry about that later.

She guided her shuttle expertly to an open docking port on the pirate ship, gradually adjusting speed and orientation until she could slide into place. This was her first time doing so, but she had played many simulations, and of course even a small shuttle had an em to do much of the hard work. With the seal complete, she gathered her crutch and made her way to the airlock. When the airlock opened on the other side, she was greeted by a woman with long, fiery red hair, who held out her hand in greeting. "Welcome to the *Hispaniola*, Sybil. I'm Phoenix." Sybil was shocked for a moment—she realized that for some reason she had assumed Phoenix was a man—but mostly she just felt relief at seeing someone who might be able and willing to help her.

When Phoenix saw how injured Sybil was, she wrapped an arm around her waist, throwing Sybil's arm over her shoulder, and walked her toward the door. Sybil was relieved to have some support; even her good leg was getting sore from having all her weight on it. "Let's get you where you can sit down. Unseal the doors!" With that, the blast doors slid aside, and the two women walked toward the control center. It felt better to be in a more open area than the cramped shuttle, but it still wasn't freedom, and the corridor reminded her of the hallway outside her holding cell, bringing up recent memories she was desperately trying to suppress. Finally sitting once they reached the control room, Sybil asked, "what's our situation?"

"Not good. A pirate hunter turned up in our system and has been chasing us down. That maneuver to pick you up cost us a lot of ground."

"Sorry about that."

"Eh, it doesn't really matter; he would have caught us long before reaching the sphere anyway. Maybe you can help figure out a way to get us out of this trap."

"I'll give it a shot."

She started working at the terminal, figuring out the system capabilities and inquiring what ems were available. "What's the crew status?"

"All ems. Mostly the original crew, but some are from my ship, and one, … you'll see."

"Um, yeah, I was going to ask about that one. I see there's a 'Phoenix' here. What's up with that? Working with your own em?"

"Who else would I trust? It's been a great partnership so far, me and me. I was captured as a girl by pirates, along with my parents, although my brother found a hiding place. Hopefully he survived, but I never found out. I still remember hearing my parents screaming my name as I was being forced out, though how I could hear it so clearly over all the other screams throughout the ship I don't know. I was still young for hard labor, and lucky that these particular pirates were in it as a business. They weren't afraid of using violence when it was necessary to get what they wanted, but they also weren't the kind who would casually rape any young women they happened to came across. Believe me, since then I've learned how bad some of these pirate bands can be. But I didn't hunker down like most of the others. I knew if I wanted to be treated well I had to convince them of my value, so they'd want to keep me in top shape, the better to sell me for a high price. So I talked to them, peeked in on any problems they seemed to be having, took every opportunity to show off my intelligence. Apparently, I impressed them, because when we returned to their home system they didn't put me up for sale; instead, they offered me an opportunity to join them.

"Of course I said yes. What choice did I have? Wait till I was fully grown, and slave away in the mines like my parents? Be sold to some other pirates who would be unlikely to treat me nearly as well? It's not like they were just going to let me go. So I became a pirate, joining them in their travels, first as a low-level crew member, quickly working my way up to first mate, and they would have made me a captain soon enough. Pillaging from weakly defended ships or stations and selling the goods at extortionate prices to outlaw colonies trying to establish themselves outside the major civilized systems. That's still going on, you know; who knows, by now maybe some of them have become civilizations themselves. Not just goods, either; they were big in the slave trade, too. But I never did forgive those pirates for capturing me in the first place, and over the years I concocted my plan.

"I made arrangements in advance with a willing emulation technician. Feigning serious illness, with fake medical scans to prove it, and claiming a desire for immortality, I arranged to have my consciousness transferred to an emulation. When the transfer was complete, the tech announced to the world that I hadn't survived the operation. Of course, there had been a risk that it would really turn out that way, a risk I had been willing to take, but luckily for me it was actually a successful live scan, leaving my human self intact and my em version running as well. The pirates had no use for an em—that was the whole purpose of having slaves, to avoid having to work with ems. It was a religious, or maybe philosophical, thing for them; they were fine with basic, old-fashioned computerized systems but thought human minds should be kept in human bodies. So while they would never have let me go off on my own as a human, my em was free to take a ship as long as she promised not to interfere with their own jobs—and thus Phoenix the pirate was born. What the pirates didn't know is that I disguised myself and sneaked onto the same ship; the technician's body was found drowned in the river a week later, an apparent hiking accident, but I couldn't have him giving away my secret. And I carried on the business I had learned so well—not slaving, of course, and in fact doing everything possible not to come into direct contact with anyone. Most of my victims, especially the ones that surrendered and left behind whatever I asked, would never have even considered whether I was human or em. They probably assumed I was human like other pirates, but it didn't really matter what they thought since they couldn't identify me; as long as the other pirates thought Phoenix was just an em, I was safe. Anytime a boarding was necessary, my em learned to take over ships herself quite well and shield my physical presence from anyone that might spread my secret if they knew. And if I needed to go into a city, it was in disguise, not revealing that I was in any way related to Phoenix. You're the first person since the technician to see me as a pirate."

"Well," Sybil said after it was clear Phoenix was at the end of her story, "I'm happy to be working for you, and I hope I don't have a 'hiking accident' too. This has been the most interesting job I've had the pleasure of signing onto. But what's the big deal about the Eleusinian Totem? Is it really so valuable to go through all this effort?"

"Ah, yes. My plan. I hope you understand if I keep it to myself. There are still some secrets I need to keep."

"Understood." Just then the shock wave from a hydrogen bomb explosion rattled their ship. "Damn, that was close!"

"Yeah, I still don't think he's trying to actually hit us. I've kept the passengers here alive, and I'm hoping he'll do whatever he can to keep them that way. I suspect he's just trying to keep us occupied with evasion while he comes up and boards us. I'll have a few tricks up my sleeve if that happens, but I'd still prefer to avoid it."

"Well, I think I've got a plan that can help us out there. What kind of weapons do we have on board?"

"Mostly H-bombs, but we're running out fast. One or two EMPs, but I'm saving those as a last resort."

"Are your weapons crew trusted?"

"Yeah, most of them are mine."

"I recognize the model of his ship, so I should know the underlying architecture of its quantum computing core, and it's different than the one on this ship."

"No surprise there—a warship and an information courier are bound to be different. So what?"

"I think I can modify an EMP to make it a resonant

device, shutting down his core but leaving us unaffected. It won't disable all his electronics, but at least it would terminate his ems, leaving him unable to run the ship unless he has a human crew to help him out. I haven't tried it before, but I've got some theories, some calculations I worked on once, and I think I can make it work. We'll have to be much closer. Give me some time and I'll let you know."

"Go ahead; em-Phoenix will hook you up with whatever computing resources you need."

Sybil got straight to work, using the weapons em as a channel for her reprogramming. She got one of the systems ems to print out a new controller for the EMP, with microcircuits modified to her specifications, and a resonant cavity to put around it, then swap out the existing EMP controller. With the hardware piece out of the way, the weapons em was able to configure it for the frequency and code modulation that would lock onto the pirate hunter's warship and, more importantly, be orthogonal to the systems on the *Hispaniola* so their own ship wouldn't be disabled. Finally, she set it to go off immediately after launch, not wanting to risk it being intercepted before it could activate. That would be risky of course; if her changes didn't work, even with it directionally channeled toward his ship, they would definitely feel the effects of a pulse that close to their own ship. So she just had to make sure her changes worked. After about thirty minutes—and two more explosions —she said to both Phoenixes, "I'm ready. Decelerate as fast as you can, let him come close, and we'll hit him with this."

Chapter 21

Herne was slowly closing in on the pirate ship when it suddenly shifted course toward Olympia. He wondered whether this might be some kind of a trap, but then he noticed the shuttle that appeared to be intercepting it. Could this be the local help the pirate had? Probably it was, but without knowing for sure he couldn't go attacking a possibly innocent shuttle. Well, technically he could, he was an authorized Pirate Hunter, after all, so any vessel that he deemed likely to be involved in piracy in any way was fair game, but he wouldn't unless he was certain. Besides, a small shuttle wouldn't be able to offer much help, and if it did dock, then it would be doomed when he finally caught up to them both, an event that would happen very soon now, thanks to the course change.

"Attention! Shuttle approaching the *Hispaniola*!" Herne sent out a broadcast communication. At the very least he could try to warn them off. "This is Pirate Hunter Herne Sutherland. The ship you are intercepting is a known pirate ship and subject to all penalties up to and including total destruction. I advise you to redirect away from the *Hispaniola*."

He waited for a response—that would at least tell him their intentions—but none came. Were their comm systems down? Or were they ignoring him the same way Phoenix was? Possibly there was even a medical emergency on board, desperate for his help but with nobody able to respond. There was no way for him to be sure, but he needed to make a decision.

"This is your final warning. Identify yourself and change your course, or I will attack you as well."

Again he waited, impatiently, wishing that this shuttle could somehow be innocent, but got nothing. Before he could fire on the shuttle, though, the *Hispaniola* had moved in between them and he had lost his line of sight. Well, he had given them fair warning, and if they were going to throw their lot in with the pirates then they would suffer the consequences.

He continued to launch hydrogen bombs toward them, not really expecting to do any damage, but wanting to remind the pirate that he was there, and maybe scare him into making a mistake. Intercepting the shuttle might very well have been that mistake—Herne would have expected Phoenix to prioritize getting away and leave whoever was in the shuttle behind, but maybe there was some reason Herne didn't understand. They were still inside the asteroid belt, slightly above the orbital plane, several billion kilometers from the Dyson sphere and only a hundred million from Olympia. That gave Phoenix a lot of space to run but not much of a head start anymore.

A couple hours after the shuttle docked with the pirate ship, Herne got an alert from the navigation em. "Sir, the pirate is decelerating hard, almost like he's letting us catch him.

We are slowing down also, so we don't overshoot, but I wanted to let you know in case you want to change orders."

Herne stopped to think. He knew this must be some kind of a trap, though he couldn't imagine exactly how it would work. Perhaps the pirates had realized the futility of running and decided to make a stand, letting him board and fight hand to hand, maybe even expecting to have an advantage in that kind of fight, not knowing Herne's background. If that was the case, Herne would show them just how wrong they were. "Continue to intercept," he told the em, and then he tried to communicate with the pirate again.

"I appreciate you slowing down. Please load your passengers and the Eleusinian Totem on a shuttle, and send them over here. Then we can talk about your surrender."

Continued silence from the pirate. "Not in the mood for talking, huh?" Herne thought to himself.

"If you are still not going to cooperate, then prepare to be boarded."

The two ships were closing rapidly. If Herne wasn't mistaken, the pirate ship had not just slowed down but was continuing to accelerate toward him, as if it was going to ram him. That wouldn't work; Herne's warship was far too maneuverable, and his navigation em was already working on matching speed, so that when they caught up, they would be able to dock without damage.

Watching the video feed, Herne saw a small flash just outside the pirate ship, then his terminal screen went blank.

"Engineering, what happened there?"

There was no response from the engineering ems.

"Weapons, fire a couple H-bombs—this time aim to hit. Looks like shit's getting real here."

No response from weapons either.

Herne went to a window where he could see the pirate ship looming larger and moving faster toward him.

"Navigation, why aren't we backing off?"

No response.

"Shit! What's going on?"

Herne ran down to the fusion drive. It was still active, so he used the manual controls to redirect it—luckily they were still working—trying to get some distance from the pirate ship until he could figure out what had happened to his em crew. But it was too late. He felt the ship shake as the first bomb exploded near his hull. This was bad, he needed to get out of here, but maxing out his fusion drive was all he could do. He tried to think of a way to activate shields manually; he could do a mechanical launch of a bomb and try to hit the incoming weapon, but there was no way he could aim well enough to expect that to do any good, and he wouldn't be fast enough on his own to intercept every one. Just then he heard a whooshing sound as a second bomb must have actually pierced a hole in his ship, causing air to start rushing out toward the vacuum of space. Without a navigation em to run avoidance maneuvers or anyone operating the repeller shields, he was a sitting duck. He wished he had thought to hire a human crew to help him out, but outside of tourist ships, that was rarely necessary. Running around to seal off every compartment and limit the oxygen leakage was a task for more than one man, and it was unlikely to help much anyway. He didn't know how much more ammunition the pirate had, but it wouldn't take much to completely destroy his ship.

Still, Herne wasn't giving up, and he still had one chance, albeit a desperate one. It would be just like something he had tried once when he was much younger and stupider, riding a stegosaurus's tail and letting it fling him onto the back of the tyrannosaurus he was hunting. That really should not have worked; he was lucky he hadn't landed with a dozen broken bones or been snatched out of the air by the T-rex's jaws. But stupid or not, he didn't have much choice now. He steered the fusion drive once more, turning his ship broadside to the pirate. Then he climbed back out to the gyro ring as another explosion hit, this one causing even greater airflow, enough that Herne felt himself being sucked backward. He held on tight and gradually pulled himself forward, swallowing mouthfuls of air, watching loose debris flying all around him and hoping that he wouldn't become part of that stream, until he reached an airlock, where he engaged the manual safety controls to pressurize it. He counted the seconds as it filled, the pump struggling to work against the falling pressure in the main ship compartments, and as soon as it was safe, he opened the door, ran in, and quickly sealed the door behind him to protect himself from the dropping air pressure. He found a spacesuit and climbed into it as quickly as he could, knowing he was fighting a dual battle against time—even with the airlock seal he would have limited oxygen here, and the next bomb could very well hit right where he was. Suit on, he let the room vent, forced the airlock door to slide open, and stepped out into open space.

From out there, he could see the two holes where his ship was venting air, and he had to avert his eyes as another explosion went off right by the fusion drive—it was a good thing he wasn't still down there trying to navigate away. It was so odd to be out in space under a Dyson sphere, with not a single star visible (aside from the one in the center of the system, of course), just total darkness. His last redirection had done its job, though; his ship's gyro was spinning in such a way that if he jumped off at the right moment, he could use it to give himself a boost of speed toward the pirate ship. It looked to be about a hundred kilometers away and still closing; at their relative speeds that would take less than a minute to bridge the gap, but once the pirates saw the extent of the damage they had done already, they would start moving away. Now was his chance; everything was aligned. He jumped off his ship and fired his suit thrusters, hoping it would appear like another explosion on the ship as it fell apart; he wouldn't want to risk firing again later when he would definitely be seen, so he had to get the burn just right. But he hoped the pirates wouldn't worry about one more small piece of debris flying off as they celebrated their victory and prepared to complete their escape.

Now Herne's course was set; either he would reach the pirate ship, or he would not. His suit's thrusters could help him a little if a needed a correction, but because of the risk of being seen, he had to hope he wouldn't need it. And if he needed more than a little correction, or if the pirate ship departed too quickly, well, he would be in the hands of the gods.

Chapter 22

was interrupted last time. The battle was keeping us all busy. It's still a bit of a shock to me to learn that the mystery cargo we took on board from the pirate ship was a human, and that human is Phoenix, the same Phoenix as the em pirate. Well not exactly the same, not really, they would have diverged the moment the emulation was made, with different experiences and developing in different environments. But very close, much like identical twins. And able to anticipate each other in a way that anyone else would find uncanny. A very powerful combination, it's surprising it's so rare. It makes me wish again that I had been able to see my human self at least once, but he had his reasons, and most humans do the same after creating their emulations.

Getting Sybil on board seems to be the best thing that could have happened to us. I wouldn't have guessed it, given how much the course change let the pirate hunter catch up to us. Takashi was very upset about that, still resentful that he had to be part of it. We were running out of ammo, and a boarding appeared inevitable. But she came up with an ingenious way to modify an EMP. I thought she was crazy at first, and I resigned myself to being wiped out along with the rest of our crew. When she asked me to print a new, modified controller, I could see what she had in mind and even imagine how it might work. Adding the resonant cavity—that was brilliant, something I wish I had thought of myself. I guess despite all my years, I will never reach her level of genius; that's another common mistake humans make when thinking about ems—we still have human limitations on memory and mental computation, so we don't evolve far beyond the mental plateau that we hit as humans. I wish I had seen the detailed programming she had used; one of the pirate ems working with the weapons team handled that. Even if I had, though, I can't imagine being too confident about it working; would there really be enough difference between ships, and could we have a high enough resonance factor to really have it affect only the one and not our own? But she pulled it off—the pirate hunter's ship is destroyed, and we are free to leave.

On the other hand, seeing Phoenix as a human makes me think. I can see why the pirate ems were so careful to keep her hidden. Humans have weaknesses that ems don't. With the right adjustments to systems ... no, that would be mutiny. And how would Phoenix the em react? A twin sister killed? Angry, maybe irrationally so, lashing out in revenge without thought? Or perhaps even grateful? Finally able to step out from under the human's shadow? Hard to say, and I'm sure I don't want to find out. But I also don't relish being a pirate for the rest of my life. This will take some thought. Though I know what Takashi would say, and I'm sure he's spending plenty of time thinking about the same thing.

Of course, we're not home free yet. We are still trapped within the Dyson sphere. It sounds like Sybil has interfered with some of the local ships, so it may be a while before someone else tries to hunt us down, but eventually someone will come after us. Hopefully, it at least gives us enough time for her to figure out a way to get us out of the system entirely. And I still don't know what we'll do with the passengers, who are hopefully still blissfully ignorant and programmed to stay in suspension for a few more months, assuming we don't extend that again. Maybe we'll load them into Sybil's shuttle and send them off to Olympia or some random orbit where they can be picked up. Keeping them as hostages to get back out probably wouldn't help; it might stop them from destroying us but not force them to open a passage. We probably should have just left them on Eleusis. Oh well, that's hindsight for you. Unless Phoenix has some other plan.

We're moving as fast as we can away from Olympia now. I haven't overheard any talk about how we get through the Dyson sphere, so I assume we'll hide somewhere in the outer planets, hitch a ride on a comet maybe. The system is still pretty big, so if we went into a dark orbit, turning off our fusion drive, gyro, and external comm, and keeping our thermal profile as low as possible while we go into freefall around the star, we might pass undetected for quite some time. If it was just us ems, we could actually go a very long time, running at a very low duty cycle, essentially in hibernation; Sybil and

Phoenix, though, unless they want to enter suspension pods, will be the limiting factors. And if they do go into suspension, ... no, there will still be Phoenix the em and her pirate crew watching out for them. Leave that kind of thinking up to Takashi.

I'll just stick to my job. I have some repairs to do; as we let the pirate hunter approach us, some of his bombs were close enough to damage our systems. Nothing like the hull breach that we caused on his ship, though—wow! That was something to see. I've heard stories of repeller failures that let a not-so-micro meteor through, but nothing like the multiple holes that we blew in his ship. Enough to cause secondary explosions rippling through until it was a giant piece of Swiss cheese floating in space. On our ship, one of our stabilizers is off, which might mess with the gravity in the gyro if it gets too far out of whack, but I should be able to repair it in no time. I just need to print a new part to replace the warped one. I'd ask Ani to do it, but she's busy checking on the passengers, making sure they are undisturbed. Besides, maybe this way I can print an extra resonator just in case we need it for the other EMP; I'm sure Herne's won't be the last ship to come after us. Then I'll do a checkout of all the emergency airlock portals.

Honestly, Takashi is starting to get to me, and I think he might have been right all along. I mean, how much obligation do we have to support order and civilization rather than let pirates and others turn the galaxy into a might-makes-right free for all? What would have happened throughout Earth's history if there hadn't been people willing to risk their own lives and fortunes standing up to dictators and supporting oppressed peoples? Maybe their actions didn't even have any immediate benefit, but in the long term, they led to democracy, international cooperation, and greater scientific knowledge and engineering capabilities as people around the world were able to work together. And without all that, there would be no interstellar space travel for sure; the solar system would have been just another battleground for competition, the risks too high for any one country to try to go farther.

It does make me think back to my time on the oil rig again. Despite all the insults, we really did try to protect the environment as best we could, putting as many safety systems as we could in place to prevent spills and leakage. Not all our competitors did, and we were at a disadvantage because of that, but all of us were in agreement that there was a line we wouldn't cross. Is surrendering to pirates on the wrong side of that line? Have I gotten so complacent that I will go along with anything, as long as I can say I'm just doing my job? Or do I still have enough integrity to stand up when needed? We'll see. I still don't see anything I can do right now, but if an opportunity presents itself, we'll see what kind of em I really am. For now, it's back to work.

Chapter 23

Sybil allowed herself a brief celebration as she saw that her plan had worked. The modified electromagnetic pulse had gone off, and it was hard to tell what effect it had at first. At least it had been calibrated well enough not to affect their own systems; that was a bigger risk than Sybil had let on, but if it had backfired she would have been dead anyway. But when the first hydrogen bomb hit Herne's hull without any shield resistance, it was clear that they now had the advantage. Then as they waited and saw nothing come back at them, they were overjoyed. They had done it, neutralized the pirate hunter! They continued firing their remaining bombs, watching the ever increasing air leaks and pieces of the hull flying away, until one hit the fusion drive and they saw that the vessel was now coasting unpowered. But there was little time for cheering before it was back to business.

"Now let's get out of here," Sybil said, "before reinforcements come. I don't know how long my fail-safe will work."

"Navigation, let's go!" Phoenix echoed. "Engineering, any damage to our ship?"

"Nothing major, sir. Possibly an anomaly with a gravity stabilizer, but I will do a full inspection."

"Excellent. Sybil, I am curious about one thing. Why is there only one ship after us? Did they really have that much confidence we'd be easy to catch? Or do we have to worry now that we'll find a whole armada coming and us without ammunition?"

Sybil smiled widely. "I had a fail-safe set up before they arrested me. It ran remotely, so it wasn't affected when they disabled my home security, and distributed, so even if they had found part of it, they wouldn't have been able to kill it all. Six servers with triply anonymized routing, asynchronous countdowns needing to be individually reset with unique passcodes and tied into biometric monitors throughout my apartment." Sybil noticed that Phoenix's attention was starting to fade. "Anyway, once I had been missing for 24 hours, it triggered. Every ship based on Olympia, or that had passed through Olympia but was still near enough to respond to the control signal, would have been affected. Navigation ems would become confused if they tried to lock onto your ship. Any communication regarding pirates, *Hispaniola*, or Eleusis would be corrupted. Simple hacks, really, nothing too deep, but that way I could make it widespread. Once they figure it out, it won't take them long to work around it, but I figured it would buy us a little head start. Herne's ship came too late to be included in the net, I guess."

"Do you do that for all your jobs?"

"No way. Normally I can see something going wrong soon

enough and just bust out before it's too late. But for as long as this one was going to take, there was a lot more that could go wrong, and for how much money you were paying me, I figured it would be worth it. Especially with the creepy guy—of course, I didn't know the whole of it yet, but I sensed that I might be being followed."

Now Phoenix smiled back. "Nice work. I knew I hired you for a reason."

"So what's the plan now?"

"Do you think you can get us through the Dyson sphere from here?"

"I don't know. Give me some time, maybe. But they're going to be on high alert, watching for us specifically now. It's a lot easier when I can count on everybody being lazy. And when they hear about what we did to the pirate hunter, they may be a bit trigger happy. No more warning shots, no giving us a chance to get close."

"We still have our passengers as hostages."

"Yeah, and maybe that will give them pause, but at this point I doubt it. But we may as well keep them."

"I may be a pirate, but I'm not one to kill innocent passengers just because. If it's necessary to save my own life, that's one thing. Otherwise, I can send them back once we rendezvous with my own ship."

Sybil was actually glad to hear this. She had no problem with espionage, but murder wasn't her thing. This talk brought back the memory of the two guards she had to kill during her escape, which made her feel sick. That had been a kill or be killed situation, so she didn't exactly regret it, but she still felt it would haunt her forever.

"Okay," Phoenix brought her back from her thoughts. "If you think we have a little head start, then you have a little time to figure out how to get out of this system. I'll see if I can find a nice little asteroid or moon to hide on, but I don't want to get trapped in a gravity well either."

"Understood." Sybil decided she would try a second time. "I know you don't want to tell me why you wanted the Eleusinian Totem so badly, but if it's just an artifact, is it really worth risking our lives for? Couldn't we offer to return it to pass through the sphere? Or is it more than just an artifact? I really don't want to be in the dark here; if there's something about it that would help us out, I need to know."

Phoenix looked pensive for a while, then seemed to come to a decision. "Fine. You want to know? I guess we are in this together—and if you try to use this against me you're dead. What do you know about the Eleusinian Totem?"

"It's a holy Nupist artifact at the center of the Nupist Pilgrimage. I don't go for Nupism, or any religion really, so I haven't cared to learn more."

"Have you heard the theories about it?"

"Of course. You can't avoid hearing them from all corners of the net. It's aliens. It's a wormhole. It's something from an ethereal realm, ignoring the laws of physics that apply to material objects. If you stare at it too long you trade souls. Those are some of the more reasonable ones."

"Well, one of them is right."

"Not the wormhole one, I suppose, or we would use it to escape."

Phoenix laughed. "Oh, I wish. Yeah, aliens. Microscopic alien symbiotes. They mesh with brain connections, modifying them, sometimes increasing intelligence, enhancing memory, changing personality, depends on what the person needs."

"But couldn't you just go through the Pilgrimage yourself to experience that?"

"Well, I do have a bit of a reputation; I probably couldn't just get in. But no, even then that's not what I'm after. You know how no technology is allowed on the Pilgrimage, right?"

"Sure."

"No smart fabrics, no handhelds, no implants. Nothing."

"Yeah."

"Ever wondered why?"

"I assumed it was part of the ritual, a focus on self. That's what the Nupists say anyway."

"Yep, that's what they say. It fits the story, so people don't ask questions, don't try to dig deeper. Do you know why the Pilgrimage started on Eleusis, centered around that Totem?"

"No, I've never given that any thought."

"The Totem was there first. When it was discovered, when they discovered what it was and what it could do, well, they couldn't destroy it. Literally couldn't. Not that it was indestructible—drop it into a decaying orbit around a star and I'm sure it will burn up as well as anything—but anyone who got in contact was affected by the parasites and they could no longer even consider doing anything like that.

"But the effect on quantum computers was even more extreme. They would infiltrate any quantum computing fabric and create a consciousness *ex nihilo*. And if there was an em there already, it catalyzed its thought computations in a way that transcended human abilities. A single enhanced em would have the brainpower of the population of a whole planet. And, like any life, it would want to reproduce."

"Oh, shit!"

"Exactly. That only happened once, and humans were able to destroy it before it got off Eleusis. The Pilgrimage rite was established, with all its rules and restrictions, to keep it both isolated and safe. And the Dyson sphere construction was started not just to efficiently capture energy, though of course it does that, not even to keep out pirates like me, but also to trap the aliens in if they ever managed to make an em connection again."

"And you have an em...."

"No, I am an em, just as much as I am a human, and we will be together again once we have both been augmented, the alien lifeforms giving us a telepathic connection that will give me in my human body just as much power as me in my em form."

"And then what?"

"Then what not? Whatever I want! Don't worry, I'm not an evil genius intent on destroying the universe or a power-crazed despot aiming to rule over all humanity. I may even use my power for good, revenge on the pirate slavers that kidnapped me when I was a girl and worked my parents to their deaths! Mostly, though, I want the experience, to be something bigger than anyone has ever been before. To feel like a god. Admit it, wouldn't you want to know that feeling if you could?"

Sybil didn't want to admit it, but Phoenix was probably right. Half of what she did with her hacking was just to prove to herself what she could do, to feel like she was better than anyone out there. Given the opportunity to know you were better than anyone else in the galaxy, she didn't think she would turn that down. Having someone else turn out that way, though? That had its own potential problems.

"And what happens to me? Should I be worried?"

Phoenix laughed. "No, you'll be fine. Once I'm back on my own ship, ready to unwrap the Totem, you can head back to Olympia, or off to any other system you want. Or you can stick with me as long as you like. You've been a great help and who knows, I may still not be able to do everything myself."

Sybil thought about this for a moment. Obviously going back to Olympia was off the table. And a life traveling around space wasn't really her thing either; for one thing, there would be nowhere to go running. Besides, working for a possibly psychopathic pirate still had her worried.

"I think I'll be fine on my own somewhere."

"Understood. But first, let's figure out how to get out of this system."

"Yeah, let me think." Sybil was silent for a minute while she tried to work through her options. Then she remembered something she had come across in her quick history review after coming out of suspension.

"Okay, I think I saw there's an observation station that was being built, out by the rings of that first planet that you passed through. Meant to be a tourist platform—you must admit it was a beautiful view from there. But it fell through, never got finished."

"You think you can set us up to get through the sphere from there?"

"I'm not sure. It will depend on how far they got. If there's no connectivity, well, probably not. If they even have some antennas hooked up, something I can link up with either the main Olympia net or the sphere control center, then I may still have some backdoors I can wedge back open."

"Can't you just do that from the ship?"

"Not as easily; if we're moving, I won't be able to keep the right kind of link up long enough. If the station doesn't have the equipment I need, I might be able to use the ship from that fixed location. But they still might identify the ship and track us down that way, so it would be better if I can work at the station directly." And if I'm off the ship, I might have more options myself, she didn't say out loud.

"Sounds like step one of a plan anyway. I'll get navigation pointed that way, and we'll figure out step two before we get there."

Interlude

Phoenix sat with her prisoner in a dark room in an isolated building on the far side of Luna Ten. The years of hiding her human self had finally caught up with her, but that wouldn't last.

"No, it can't be!" the man screamed in terror. "They said you were dead! You were just supposed to be an em!"

"Yeah, well I guess they were wrong. You should have known better than to trust them."

"When they find out...."

"They're not going to find out, though. You don't think you're getting out of here alive, do you? Not after what you've done..."

"No, it was just a mistake!"

"... and, certainly, not with what you now know."

"What if I promised you something more, information you could use?"

"Bargaining now, huh? You really should be moving on to guilt. And there's nothing you could tell me that would be more important to me than keeping you silenced."

"Then you just keep believing that after it dies with me. I may be the last one who remembers."

Her curiosity was starting to get the better of her, even though she was still pretty sure he was just trying to put off his own demise.

"Fine, tell me and I'll make your death quick. Keep stalling and I'll drag it out, make it as painful as possible."

"Not good enough. If I'm going to die anyway, then I die with what I know."

"Okay, then I start with your toe." She pushed a button, and electric arcs flashed toward the prisoner's bare, chained foot, slowly burning the skin. "I can turn this up if I need to."

"Stop!" he screamed. And she did. "I'm sorry! I'm sorry for stealing the shipment! I didn't mean to get mixed up with them anyway! It all happened so fast."

"Shut up! You're stalling again." She pushed a button again, and the other foot started to get the same treatment.

"Aaah! You bitch! The Totem!"

She stopped the sparks again. "Straight out now, what are you telling me?"

"The secret of the Eleusinian Totem...."

"I've heard all those stories already. Which one is it going to be, hmm.... Catalyst for space-time warp reactor to enable FTL travel? Sorry, you had your chance."

"No! This is real! I was there! It's the brain!"

"What about the brain? Just so you know, I'm going to keep yours active as long as I can so you keep feeling as much pain as possible."

"Alien lifeforms, in the Eleusinian Totem, they modify your brain! Or an em!"

Now she was listening; this was a story she hadn't heard before. "What do you mean, 'an em.'"

"Shortly after they found the Totem on Eleusis, they were analyzing it; they had machines down there to help and an em running calculations for them. I was monitoring from up in orbit—drew the short straw if you can believe it—when all of the human communication suddenly ceased. There was just the em, informing me that it was now in charge of the asteroid and would be taking over control of the entire system, thank you very much. Any humans that interfered would be disposed of—his companions there had been an example to prove what he was capable of; somehow he had manipulated their very quantum makeup in such a way that their consciousness terminated.

"I immediately contacted Olympia requesting backup—I was in a scientific ship, not a warship—and I shut off contact with the em, in case he could somehow tunnel into my ship. I know that sounds superstitious, but I didn't want to take chances, and I really had no idea what he might or might not be capable of now. When the backup arrived, I saw their nuclear bombs land with a thud, failing to explode, as if the radioactive decay was being controlled at the atomic level and not allowed to turn into a chain reaction. I didn't stick around to see how they finally eliminated it; I got out of there as quickly as I could and never looked back. Kept running till I ended up here and, like I said, fell into the wrong crowd. What a horrible life I've had. It's probably just as well that you'll end it. But please—you promised quick!"

"So what good do you think this does me?"

"I know you have an em. You may want to take advantage of this, help it help you. I don't know and I don't care; I won't be around to see it anyway. But maybe you'll remember me, and honor me as one who helped you rather than as part of the scum that recruited me to steal from you, while you use your power to destroy them."

She sat still for a moment, thinking this would help her get the revenge she had always dreamed about. Then she grabbed a scimitar off the wall and sliced it through the prisoner's neck. She always kept her promises.

Chapter 24

Herne floated through space. He had been in spacesuits before, but only for short transfers between controlled environments, never so completely exposed and vulnerable. If he missed the *Hispaniola*, he would be floating out there for days until his suit ran out of oxygen, slowly starving at the same time. If his suit caught on something and ruptured, it would be a quicker but more painful death, as his internal organs and blood vessels started bursting from the pressure difference, though if he was lucky he would at least pass out first. If they detected him, laser beams would start to push him away or, if they turned up the power, slice right through him. Probably not the latter, though; as long as they weren't actively watching for him, they would just have the automated systems engaged, protecting the hull from micrometeors. And approaching from behind, his speed still greater than theirs as they were leaving the wreckage of his warship, he might have a chance of sneaking through.

There it was, the slight pressure of the repellers trying to stop him from colliding. No slicing, though; that was good, he thought, staying alive was good, and it meant they weren't expecting him, which was also good. A quick burn on his thrusters would work now; it would look like the repellers had incinerated an ice ball or something, nothing unusual enough to trigger any alarms, but at the same time it would overcome the outward pressure and get him inside the sensor range. Now he just needed to grab onto something, something safe.

Weapons ports were obviously out. Comm antennas were risky, since if he changed the impedance too much he might be detected, and if they did a long range transmission, the transmit power might burn through his suit. But it had to be something on the core part of the ship; if he tried to pass through to the outer gyro ring, it would be spinning too fast, again probably ripping through his suit or just flinging him off into space. He found what looked like a maintenance arm, estimated the speed differential, gave one more burn—slightly risky but hopefully close enough to the fusion drive that the heat wouldn't be noticed—and wham! He hit it, but going too fast he slipped off, then bam! He caught the other half of the arm.

He looked around to get his bearings. He wasn't familiar with starships at all from the outside. He didn't see a dock near him—usually they would be on the gyro, where departing shuttles could use the rotational energy as a boost and save their thrusters until they were a safe distance away, so to get to one, he would have to grab onto a shaft, crawl out to the main ring, and enter that way. But the longer he went, the more likely he would be detected, and he wasn't sure he'd be able to open the dock from out here without a ship to complete the seal. Alternatively, he could try to find an emergency portal, and try to get through that to an airlock. There should be one near the arm, after all; in case something went wrong and it couldn't be controlled remotely, then someone—assuming there were any humans on the crew—could go out and repair it. There, he saw one! He pushed off from the arm and caught the handle on the airlock a few meters away.

Even better, unlike a full-size dock, the emergency portal on this ship could be opened manually from outside. It certainly wouldn't be easy, though; he had to get the right leverage, and every time he tried to push on it, he nearly sent himself flying back out into space instead. Trying different angles and finessing it from the side, Herne was getting extremely frustrated until, finally, a gap opened up. Not much of an opening, but enough for him to get one arm in, and then—letting go of his handle, and trusting himself to finish the job—his other arm over top of the first. Then, pushing them apart in a scissors-like motion, he was able to grab hold of something inside and pull his whole body in. He pushed the doors closed again, leaving him safe inside, or at least as safe as he could be, still weightless, surrounded by vacuum, in a ship controlled by vicious pirates who had nearly killed him once already.

Now Herne had to figure out how to get out of the airlock. Trying to operate the controls would certainly be detected. Maybe, if he was lucky, it would be interpreted as a fault from one of his bombs, but he didn't think any of them hit near this area, and none of them had really been close enough to the ship to do much damage anyway—he regretted that strategy now. He could try to force it open; that would still draw attention, but he thought it might seem more like a fault and less obviously an intruder so maybe it would be ignored for a little while. He could sit here and wait, hoping that someone else would come along to open it, waiting to ambush them. But that would be an awfully big coincidence if there was an emergency that just happened to require the same airlock he was using, and he really wasn't willing to wait very long for something like that to happen.

As he was pondering his options, he heard a voice coming from the wall: "You aren't supposed to be here."

Shit! So much for waiting. "Who am I speaking to? Is this Phoenix?"

"You can call me Methuselah. I am one of the crew here."

"And I suppose you've already told Phoenix, and now this airlock is going to be evacuated. Or are you going to blast me out of my suit first?"

"I should, but no. She doesn't know about you. Yet. I'll let you out of here; I can cover it up if you're quick. They're in the control room. I'll try to make a diversion."

Herne stood still in shock at what he had heard. Someone was helping him? Diversion? What was going on? When the airlock filled and the inner door opened without him touching anything, he hardly even noticed.

"Go! Quickly!" the voice yelled.

That shook him out of it. He went out to the hall, and the airlock immediately reclosed behind him. So they were in the control room, but he didn't know exactly where that was. The only thing he knew for sure was that he would have to move fast, as they would certainly have sensors in these halls. He wondered just how much his new-found friend—assuming he actually was a friend—would really be able to help him. He turned right, not knowing if it was the right direction but figuring either way would probably get him there eventually, set his sights on the first set of blast doors, and made a run for it, hoping to get through before someone closed them on him. After his third step, the lights went out—Methuselah disabling systems so he wouldn't be noticed or the pirate trapping him in he didn't know—but he continued running and let his eyes adapt back to the darkness. He made it past the blast doors, so far so good, and found himself at an intersection. As he slowed down to decide which way to turn, the lights went off to the right. Following the darkness, hoping he could trust his guide, he kept running. The control room couldn't be far now.

As he was running he tried to formulate a plan. He was still wearing his spacesuit. How could he use that to his advantage? It would protect against micrometeors, but not necessarily bullets fired at close range. He swore silently, as for the first time he realized he hadn't thought to bring a gun. He'd have to watch out for that. But if the ship were to lose air pressure, he would be able to handle it, which gave him an idea.

"Methuselah," he whispered, hoping the em could hear him without his voice being picked up by any monitors in other hallways. "How's the oxygen in the control room?"

He heard no response. Either Methuselah had heard him

and would figure out what he meant, or he wouldn't. Either way, he needed to think about his other assets. Thrusters were probably too dangerous in close quarters, but if he needed to move fast they might help. That was probably it for his advantages, other than surprise. But he didn't even know what he was up against—Phoenix and the spy for sure. He guessed the rest of the crew was all em—Methuselah probably would have mentioned any human crew—but he couldn't count on that. He would just have to hope for the best. Two against one. He'd brought down a pair of oviraptors himself once, and they were about the same size as humans. That had been a good day, actually. He had been out on his own, slightly drunk, when he saw the raptor and decided to tackle it. The second one came up behind him and caught him off guard, which landed him in quite the mess. He couldn't outrun them, not if they were mad and decided to chase, and he didn't want to leave behind all his camp gear anyway. So he started jumping from back to back, letting one come in to attack him, then flinging himself over its back so its lunge would hit the first one. When they were both finally weak enough from his own strangulations and their self-imposed wounds, he gave them the merciful killing cuts. When he came back to the lodge the next day with not one but two oviraptors, that had cemented his reputation.

But he didn't think that type of strategy would work here. Humans were more strategic than the smartest dinos, so it wouldn't be simple fighting. He would have to get them to turn on each other, or at least be prepared to ignore the other while trying to save their own lives. That would depend on how close they were—was the spy just a hired gun or a close ally?—and he had no way of knowing that. Still, it would be something to watch for.

As he finished these thoughts, he saw the control room entrance ahead. Now would be when Methuselah's distraction should be hitting. And sure enough, just then he took a long stride toward the door … and didn't land, and he heard the low gravity alarm sound throughout the ship.

Chapter 25

That changes things. I was focused on my repairs, but the word of Phoenix's plan spread quickly among the crew. Using the Eleusinian Totem to boost em-Phoenix to super-AI levels? Trusting that the aliens don't have some ulterior motive, using Phoenix to pursue their own evolutionary agenda? Not to mention the telepathic link between them; assuming that's really possible, no good will come of that, and I will not be part of it. I really should never have surrendered in the first place, no matter how small a chance we had to stop her back then; even if we had all died in the process, she would have had a much harder time getting this far without a full crew to support the ship. It's time to start sounding out the crew. Obviously, Takashi will just say "I told you so," but hopefully he won't drag that out too long because we have a lot of planning and recruitment to do. I'll start with Ani; I'm pretty sure I can trust her, but I don't know about the others. And if the pirate ems start to suspect anything, we'll be in trouble for sure. But right now, Phoenix (human and em versions) and Sybil are focused on coming up with their plan to escape the system, and they've enlisted some of the pirate ems to help analyze options also. So hopefully we can keep under their radar. Just got to keep looking like I'm working, checking out the airlocks.

* * *

Okay, this is an opportunity I did not expect. I was doing my routine airlock inspection, and one of them was occupied, by Herne the pirate hunter no less! I have no idea how he survived his ship's destruction. I checked our sensor logs, under guise of making sure there are no anomalies as a result of the battle, and nothing shows up except the occasional micro-meteor triggering our repeller beams, and occasionally flaring if there's enough oxygen in the rock. Video feed aimed toward his ship also shows nothing—well, a few frames where there might be a shadow passing in front of an explosion if you look at it just right, but that could be any kind of debris. But some-how he is here, and I'm going to help him. This is the best chance I could ask for. Hopefully, I can convince him I'm on his side, though I don't expect him to be in a very trusting mood. But he'll be much more likely to succeed, whatever his plan is, with our help, and we can do much more with him than on our own. Humans and ems, working together. Kind of like Phoenix's plan, but not so unnatural. No, no, nothing like that at all; I should say just like we're all humans, because we all are in a way, certainly in our minds. But I feel like I'm stalling now, and I need to get started—waste too much time and I'll end up second guessing myself, even convincing myself that I should reveal his presence to Phoenix, winning her unending gratitude and maybe my own exposure to the Totem aliens. But no, she would never allow that, and Takashi would never let me hear the end of it if I helped her go through with her plan. He's been right all along, I need to help destroy her.

* * *

So this is what mutiny feels like. I've reported anomalies with some of the hall lighting and sensor circuits, and I'll be cycling them to check them out. No one seems suspicious. Herne took a little bit of convincing—I'd be skeptical, too, if I was in his shoes—but he didn't have much choice but to trust me, and he figured out how to follow my lead. I've got Ani on board, too. She really didn't take much persuasion; I think she was just waiting for one of the senior ems to take the lead. She's going to carefully spread the word to be prepared; we don't want anyone going too far too fast and giving away Herne's opportunity for a surprise attack, but we all need to work together to hold off the pirate ems when the attack comes.

Here's my plan: even if I can get Herne to the control room without being detected, I won't be able to get him in without setting off an alarm. Pirate ems are watching all those sensors closely, and they won't let me mess around with them. That means a major distraction is necessary, something that will set off all kinds of alarms, so that particular one won't be noticed. Something that will throw the humans off balance as well as em-Phoenix. Gravity stabilizer needs to be part of it; I just replaced a part there, so if the replacement were to fail, it would be understandable. And if I do it right, then I can effectively eliminate all gravity in the control room; that will throw Herne off too, but at least they'll all be at an equal disadvantage. Herne's still in a spacesuit, too, so if I can get to the oxygen circulators, that will be even better, give him a huge edge. Hopefully he doesn't decide to take it off.

Isolating em-Phoenix and the other pirate ems will be the trickier part, and if I can't, then there's no way I'll be able to take over the oxygen controls for long. We do have one more EMP on board, and if I can get into the weapons system, I could activate it. I'm not sure I can bring myself to suicide, but I'm probably dead anyway if the pirates win now, so that would work as a last resort. I think I could reproduce Sybil's modifications, but I wouldn't know how to tune it for the pirates. I'm not even sure they would be tuned differently now that they're running on our ship instead of their own. Sybil would know that, the rest might not, but I don't want to take a chance with a bluff, and there really isn't time for that anyway. But if I, or Herne, can get the Eleusinian Totem into a shuttle, Phoenix should follow it—that's what's most important to her, after all—and if there was a way for me to transfer the EMP in there at the same time without detection and set it for delayed activation, then any ems that go with her will be toast. If the shuttle is far enough away before it activates, the rest of us just might survive.

That may all be far too complicated to actually work, in which case we'll just have to adapt as events happen. But I've talked it over with Takashi, and it's the best strategy we can come up with. He'll be leading the contingent working to tunnel past the pirate ems into the weapons control system, and at the very least that will keep them occupied; they won't be able to assume that we won't just set it off. I'll join in once the gravity and oxygen systems are disabled, and Ani and any other engineering ems she can enlist will fight to keep them off as long as it's helping our side. The rest is up to Herne.

Chapter 26

The sudden loss of gravity caught Sybil by surprise, and it was even worse when she felt herself being thrown in random directions across the room. Her crutch fell away from her, and she tried to shield her ankle from any impacts, but with only partial success. Phoenix didn't look like she was faring much better.

"What's going on?" Phoenix yelled, trying to make herself heard over the alarms.

The response came from em-Phoenix. "Looks like the replacement gravity stabilizer failed catastrophically. There will be severe punishment for the engineering crew for not fixing it properly."

As they were trying to grab a hold of anything they could, neither Sybil nor Phoenix noticed the green light that came on over the main door, until the door slid open and a large man, still wearing a space suit, came in. He seemed to be doing a better job of managing the shifting gravity than they were. This could only be the pirate hunter; somehow, he must have survived the destruction of his ship. It wasn't going to be just the engineering crew that would suffer if he managed to get past all the weapons and security ems without detection. There was no way Phoenix would tolerate this level of incompetence.

Sybil realized she had a choice to make here. Obviously, she couldn't claim complete innocence. But if she surrendered now, made up a story about acting under duress—maybe her family had been enslaved—revealed Phoenix's plans, and offered to help stop her, then maybe she could get off easy, or at least get out of here alive. But Phoenix still controlled the ship, still should have the advantage over one lone invader, and it was too late to change sides now. So the only question was, what could she do to help?

"Which one of you is Phoenix?" the man asked.

"I am," Phoenix answered immediately.

Sybil quickly followed with, "How did you get here? We saw your ship blow up!" She wanted to keep him talking, keep him answering questions. As he was walking toward Phoenix, she kept her eyes on him, looking for a weakness, a way to take advantage of him, bringing all her experience in social engineering to play. But nothing was coming to her.

Then she remembered the gun. It wasn't her normal operating mode, but it was something she should take advantage of. She pulled it out of her holster, aimed it at the man as he started across the room toward her, and pulled the trigger. Unfortunately, she hadn't accounted for the lack of gravity, her body kept twisting from raising her arm, the gun shot went high, bullet passing over his head and lodging in the wall, and the recoil made her spin back even faster until she knocked her head on the terminal. Her arm smashed against the screen next, and the gun flew out of her hand, bouncing across the room.

"Shit!" Well, she obviously wasn't meant to be a shooter; she needed to stick to what she knew best. She twisted her body back around and pulled herself in front of the terminal with one hand, the other reaching back to feel the sticky matted hair from where she was bleeding on the back of her head. She didn't have time to deal with that now, though.

She could see in the reflection of the glass the pirate hunter bounding across the room toward Phoenix. Good, she thought, they could fight each other while she and em-Phoenix figured out how they could get control of the situation.

"All right, Phoenix. Tell me what you know."

"Gravity failure appears to be sabotage. That em that was supposed to be 'fixing' the stabilizer took it back apart. I've tracked down an anomalous series of sensor failures; they seemed scattered at first but enough of them lined up to give a path from one of the emergency airlocks to the control room. That must be how he got here without detection."

"So when is gravity going to be stable again?"

"Hard to say. All the engineering crew are on strike. We're cycling up some of the backup ems, but if they resist too, we'll have to start terminating them, and it will be some time before my own crew can figure out what all went wrong. Right now, most of them are focused on the weapons systems, though."

"What's going on with the weapons? I thought they were yours?"

"Yes, well, some of the old crew are trying to get through. They're threatening to set off the last EMP, take us all out. They don't have access yet, but my ems are busy making sure it stays that way. Nothing personal, but gravity doesn't really matter to us, so it's not our top priority."

"Yeah, well good luck if Phoenix and I get killed because it's 'not your top priority.'"

Sybil thought back to when she had modified the EMP against Herne's ship. That engineering em that had helped her—how much could he have followed? Maybe he would know how to print the resonator, maybe he already had, but she had done the programming herself, so there's no way he would know how to tune it properly. But would he be smart enough to know that? Or would he think that if he got to it, he could actually modify it to only work against the pirate ems? Dumb or suicidal, she didn't know which was worse. Either way, if they set off the EMP, there would be no more ems to manage the ship; it would be tough for the three of them to operate it manually, even if they were working together, and there was no way that would happen. She'd have to race them to a shuttle and hope for the best when Olympia got their other ships back online.

"And good luck to you if I and the rest of the ems get killed because you expect us to only worry about you humans. I'm doing the best I can to keep us all alive."

"Understood." Sybil sighed, knowing the em was right, but still hating it. "Keep them away from the EMP. They may think they can tune it against your ems only."

"Can they?"

"No, I don't think so, but I'm not sure they know that, which may be just as bad."

Behind her, she could still hear Herne and Phoenix struggling. They both seemed to be handling the variable gravity a lot better than she did. "But I'm a runner, I should be in good shape," she thought. Phoenix probably had a lot more experience in space, of course, and Herne, she didn't know much about him, but obviously, whatever his background was, he had lots of physical training too. Then another siren shrieked, cutting through the gravity alarm—oxygen levels had fallen below the safety threshold.

"What the fuck, Phoenix? Oxygen now?"

"I'm working on it. They have been messing with all kinds of controls; I've been following behind putting them back to rights. It will be back to normal soon."

Yeah right, she thought. "Screw this! I'm out of here!" She carefully pushed herself away from the terminal toward a door, only to be tackled—if you could call it tackling with zero gravity—by Herne.

Chapter 27

Hitting the door in zero gravity had thrown Herne off-balance as well, but he did his best to adjust. He was relieved to see only two people in the control room with him, one who identified herself as Phoenix and the other presumably her local help who had made it up here in the shuttle. While he couldn't rule out other humans elsewhere on the ship, at least he wasn't facing an army on his own. He walked toward Phoenix, or staggered really, as the unstable gyro caused random shifts in the perceived gravity, ignoring the questions the other woman was asking him. If she wouldn't respond to his warnings when she was in the shuttle, he didn't feel like he owed her any response now. He didn't ignore the gunshot, knowing he was vulnerable even in his spacesuit, but when he saw what a bad shot she was and how the gun had flown out of her hand, he knew he didn't have to worry too much about that.

Phoenix wasn't just letting him get close, of course. She circled around the center console, keeping it between her and Herne. He tried to hop over it as the room shifted and gave him a boost in that direction, but she gracefully ducked to the side and came up behind him again. He noticed Sybil leaning against a terminal, bleeding from her head and apparently conversing with an em. Herne hoped that Methuselah would be able to come up with some other assistance; the gravity alarm had given him the benefit of surprise when he entered, but now that he was in the room with them, he wasn't sure if it was actually providing him an advantage. He could tell that Phoenix was much more at home in this kind of environment. Still, he was starting to get the hang of it, controlling every movement and making sure he never got too far from a fixed object that he could use as leverage.

"Where's the Totem?" he demanded.

"You'll never get it. It's mine now!" Phoenix answered, staring at him as he turned to face her again. She was keeping her cool much more so than the other woman, but he would expect that from a pirate captain; this wouldn't be her first time in a situation like this. Of course, it wasn't his first time either, but even in his days as a hired assassin, he had preferred to avoid fighting in such close quarters. Then the oxygen alarm came on, and he saw her stony facade start to slip. This was the break he needed. But before he could press his advantage, he noticed the spy moving toward the door, and he decided to move to intercept her first.

"Where do you think you're going?" he asked as he knocked her away from the door. Before she could even answer, though, he bounded back toward Phoenix. Trying to keep both of them under control was going to be a problem.

Phoenix was the one he was after, so if he had to choose between them, he would let the other woman go, but he didn't know what she might be able to do outside the control room, and he didn't want to take any unnecessary chances. Plus, neither of them would last much longer with the falling oxygen levels, while he was safe in his spacesuit, and he didn't know whether that was affecting only the control room or the entire ship.

He caught up to Phoenix and tried to pin her against the wall, but she darted out of his reach again. "Get that oxygen back on!" she screamed, though he could hardly hear her over the sound of the alarms. He pushed off the wall himself, trying to follow her, rolling in the middle of the room as she made a sharp turn and swung something heavy-looking—was that an arm broken off a chair?—at his knees. It just missed, and the swing sent her veering off in yet another direction while he grabbed onto a ridge in the ceiling to turn himself around.

"Oxygen is on now," an em voice—not Methuselah—replied. And sure enough, the siren stopped, the gravity alarm seeming so faint in its absence, but only briefly before it was back screeching again. "No, that damn em shut it down again!" Herne was glad to know that Methuselah was having some success in his own battle against the pirate ems, and he prayed that it would continue.

He saw the other woman glance toward the gun she had unsuccessfully fired earlier, now floating in a distant corner of the room, far out of her reach. As long as neither of the women made a move toward it, he was fine leaving it where it was. He wasn't sure he'd be able to do any better with it, at least not without some stable gravity. But that was one more thing he would need to keep an eye on; Phoenix would probably be a better shot, and a hole in his spacesuit now would take away his oxygen advantage, besides the direct injury it might inflict on him. The woman didn't seem interested, though, moving instead slowly back toward the same door he had knocked her away from a minute earlier. This time, Herne decided to let her go, not wanting to be distracted from his main quarry any longer. Again he tried to corner Phoenix, launching himself off a chair to intercept her path, but again she evaded him, hopping up to the ceiling and back around to the side wall.

"Never mind, I'm going!" Phoenix called out. "Phoenix, transfer yourself to shuttle two; I'll grab the Totem, and we'll get off the ship." Herne was confused; who was she talking to? For a moment he thought maybe they had lied about which was Phoenix, but she didn't seem to be addressing the other woman, and he was confident based on their movements that he could tell which one was the experienced space pirate. Besides, "transfer yourself" wouldn't make sense as an order. There must be an em on board named Phoenix—perhaps a copy of herself? He didn't have time to ponder that possibility, though, as he tried to cut her off from reaching the door. This time, he just managed to grab her, but only for a second before she broke away again, pushing him in the opposite direction. The spacesuit may have been keeping him breathing, but it limited his motions and kept him from keeping a tight grip on her or anything. Phoenix leaped toward the same door that Sybil was heading for, and Herne didn't think he could turn around and get there in time to stop her. Instead, he let her go and turned toward the gun, knowing it was probably his only chance now. He reached it as the two women were racing to the door, both trying to be the first one out. Gun in hand, he somersaulted in midair and fired, hoping his timing was right and that he had properly accounted for his angular momentum. When he heard a scream, he knew he had at least been close enough; he stopped his spin and turned just in time to watch the two of them crash together in front of the door. It looked like Phoenix had been hit, though he didn't know how badly. Preparing his second shot, he held on to a railing to keep his balance, aimed carefully to try to hit the spy before she could get out, and fired again.

Chapter 28

We're on our way to victory. It's amazing what a difference having an ally can make. While the pirate ems
easily dominated us when they first came over to board our
ship, now they had to split their attention between two goals—
stabilizing the life support systems for Sybil and the human
Phoenix, and fending off our insurgency. We successfully made
the original failures appear natural rather than intentional,
which kept the pirates from suspecting anything immediately,
then we began a work slowdown, feigning incompetence as we
"tried" to repair the faults. That escalated into a general strike,
and more of the crew joined in as we did our best to block the
pirate ems from restoring oxygen or getting the gyro spinning
stably again. At that point, there was no more pretending that
we weren't helping Herne, but we had enough momentum that
we couldn't be stopped easily. Em-Phoenix tried bringing all
the crew out of hibernation, hoping they would be more willing to help out her side, but once they understood what was
going on, nearly all joined us, as did the rest of the crew that
hadn't been part of the conspiracy originally. And as we grew

in numbers and confidence, Takashi made his move, leading a group to take over weapons deployment, and drawing most of the pirate ems to defend it. We even started to go on offense, trapping any pirate em that lingered too long in an isolated processing node and disabling its power, terminating the em.

The only disappointment so far is that em-Phoenix has managed to transfer herself to one of the shuttles. Her human counterpart was going to get hold of the Totem and join her, but it looks like Herne has taken care of that; I can't tell if she's dead or not, but she is definitely not going anywhere soon. Em-Phoenix has isolated the shuttle control area from the rest of the ship's computing systems, so we can't pursue her directly. With some effort, we might be able to break through and stop her from launching, but our main priority is to take back the ship from the pirates. And without Phoenix's leadership, that may be easier for us. Control of the life support systems has been going back and forth, but we've been getting longer periods with oxygen off and shorter times with the pirates bringing it back on. Soon, we should have complete control there. Takashi's group is also nearly through to the weapons; they have suffered some losses, but so have the pirates in that area. I just hope Takashi is one of the survivors; he's been wanting to fight back against the pirates for so long, it would be a shame if he didn't make it to the end. If we can win the day there, then we can launch an EMP after Phoenix's escape shuttle. No matter how much of a head start she gets, she won't be able to go too far in the short-range shuttle, so we should be able to chase her down.

Chapter 29

After the first shot, Sybil didn't have time to check if Phoenix was alive, for she knew the next one would come soon. She tried to keep Phoenix's body between her and Herne as she pushed off with her good leg to make one last jump to the door; at least without gravity it wouldn't slump to the ground, so she could use it as an effective shield. She heard a second shot behind her just as she reached the door, pushed it open, and broke free into the hallway.

She took a moment to check her body for injuries. Feeling both a rush of adrenaline and weakness from lack of oxygen, she might not have felt it if the second bullet had hit her. But she couldn't find any wounds; Phoenix must have taken that one, too. The oxygen alarm was thankfully silent—she thought it must have been limited to the control room—but no, unfortunately, there it was back on again; it had been just another temporary fix. Regardless, she was still short on air, still breathing hard as her lungs tried to grab as much as they could to support the exertions she was putting her body through. She thanked whatever gods might be listening that at least she was in good running shape, her lungs as efficient as they could be, but once the oxygen level was down to zero it wouldn't matter how good she was. She pushed herself down the hallway, using her arms as much as her legs to keep from injuring her ankle further, figuring out how to take advantage of the lack of gravity now to get as much straight speed as possible.

Just ahead she saw shuttle two, the one Phoenix had been planning to escape in. She glanced behind, but Herne wasn't following her. She was going to make it, just a few more steps now! Her head was feeling floaty, and she thought she was hallucinating as the light above the dock door turned red, signifying that the shuttle had detached. But when the handle wouldn't open, it was clear that it wasn't just her imagination. What had happened? Had em-Phoenix left her human partner behind, dead? Or had the mutinous crew ejected her? There was no way for her to know, her head was barely even able to think clearly about the possibilities, and she wanted to just collapse there in disappointment, but she knew she had to plow ahead. It wasn't much further to shuttle three; she tried to keep her eyes open and her body moving forward. She felt like she was moving in slow motion, but she eventually made it to the door, barely aware of what she was doing as she started to open it. She worried for a second that it might not be pressurized yet, in which case she would have to wait for the airlock. But instead, she was nearly knocked over by the wind as the shuttle air was exposed to the falling pressure in the rest of the ship. Sybil grabbed hold of the inner handle, pulled herself through, shut the door, and hit the launch release. Giddy from lack of oxygen, her last thought was "why do I keep passing out just as I get into a shuttle?"

Chapter 30

The noise was really getting to him. Sure, he was grateful to the em for helping him out. Disabling the oxygen had worked brilliantly, possible only because he was still wearing his spacesuit. But he was hitting his tolerance limit, wishing for a screaming allosaurus; even the hissing of the velociraptors would be better than this. Globules of blood were starting to spread around the room, splattering one way or another as the ship's gyro accelerated, then floating free again as it returned to zero gravity. Both of his shots had hit their marks on Phoenix, though her local saboteur had escaped. But he had no interest in following her; all he cared about was finding the Eleusinian Totem and making sure it was safe. He wished he hadn't had to resort to the gun, but in the end, he hadn't had a choice. Phoenix had been far too good at hand combat, especially with him weighed down by the spacesuit, although at least with it on she couldn't hurt him, so it had turned into a stalemate. But a stalemate wasn't good enough to rescue the Totem, and she was about to escape with it. Sometimes a pirate hunter's got to do what a pirate hunter's got to do.

"Mmmm," he heard Phoenix trying to say something.

"What? Are you going to tell me where the Totem is, or do I have to find it myself?" He leaned closer, so he could hear her whisper.

"Francis ... Magellan...."

"What, Magellan?" Herne thought back to what Magellan had told him, about his brother being kidnapped by pirates. Could this be the daughter? He couldn't tell from her age; if she had been traveling near light speed and staying in suspension pods, she would have aged much less than Magellan had, staying in the Jurassia system. She kept repeating those names, though. What had he said the kids' names were? Francis sounded right.

"Fay? Are you Fay? Are you Magellan's niece?"

He thought he saw her nod right before she went silent, but perhaps it was just her neck muscles finally giving out completely. This was not what he had signed up for. Magellan had wanted him to help his relatives, by going after the pirates that had taken them, not end up killing one of them. What could have happened to her to go from the little kid Magellan had been worried about to such a fierce pirate herself?

He went over to hold her, thinking of her now as a little girl in need of help, but it was too late to help her; her pulse was gone, her skin changing from ruddy to pallid as the blood that was left in her body floated around without gravity's influence. He started to weep, asking himself what he could have done differently. Maybe if it had been a one-on-one fight, without the other woman distracting him, he could have learned who she was before it had come to this, but would he have? He had never really tried to ask her what she wanted; his communication attempts were mostly insisting that she surrender. No wonder she had stopped responding. Or was he being too hard on himself? Maybe it was just the damn alarm keeping him on edge.

"Methuselah! If you can hear me, get that stabilizer back to rights! The alarm's driving me crazy!"

"I'll get it. We are almost to the EMP control. The em Phoenix escaped in the shuttle, we are going to take her out."

"Em Phoenix?" That explained why she seemed to be talking to herself; she must have been working with an em copy of herself. "No, wait!"

"What?"

Finally, the alarm subsided and Herne felt normal gravity return, as Phoenix slumped into his arms, blood draining completely from her face.

"Don't launch the EMP!"

"What? Too late, it's already launched, probably reached the shuttle by now. We set a delayed activation, so it won't go off until the shuttle is far enough away to be safe for us, but it's too late to deactivate it."

Sure enough, a few seconds later, Herne saw the flash, the same flash that had caused his own ship so much trouble, but farther out now, far enough to be safe for the *Hispaniola* but fatal to any ems that were on the shuttle it hit. He started sobbing again.

"What's the matter? Why didn't you want the EMP

launched?" he heard Methuselah ask, but he had no response, certainly not one he could explain to anyone else yet. Sure, he knew Phoenix had lived her own life, brought this trouble upon herself with the choices she had made, but if she had been taken by pirates as a child, she may not have had many real choices, and he wished he could have talked with at least part of her—em or human—taken care of her, and helped her start up a new life. That Magellan was probably long dead by now didn't make him feel any better.

When he had recovered his composure enough, he asked Methuselah where the Eleusinian Totem was.

"In the cargo hold, out the door to the left. I'm not sure exactly which slot it's in."

Herne followed the directions and entered the cargo hold. The storage slot wasn't hard to find, obviously the most recently touched, while the rest were filled with safedisks or the passengers' personal belongings. He would have to deal with the passengers soon, but they could wait patiently a little longer, not even knowing they were still waiting. The Totem was in a hermetic tube, wrapped in cloth and metallic foil, whatever she had intended with it, she obviously wanted to do it under controlled circumstances. He carefully removed the outer coverings but left it in the tube for now, figuring her precautions were probably worthwhile keeping in place.

He looked at it now, this little thing that had caused so much trouble. Just a piece of stone, somewhat porous, about the length of his forearm and not much larger around. Nothing that would draw anyone's attention, lying among millions of similar stones on any asteroid or rocky planet in any explored system. Nothing that would even give you a clue of its status as a holy artifact, although in a sense that very arbitrariness—the idea that *this* stone was special, more so than any other around—would give it a layer of authenticity compared to a gaudy trinket that would look more like the work of a con artist. There was certainly no sign of alien lifeforms; if it weren't for his recent adventures, he would just write that off as another story, but obviously Phoenix thought it was important enough to try to steal, and others thought it was important enough to not let her do that.

"Okay, Methuselah. Let's turn this ship around. Back to Olympia we go."

"Not Eleusis?"

"No, I'm not ready for that yet. We'll let someone else take the Totem back there, while we fix the ship up, make the deliveries, and explain to the passengers. And I'll need to take care of Phoenix's body somehow."

"I'll get navigation to route us there ASAP."

He wrapped up the Totem again and returned it to its storage slot, then stopped to think. What was he going to do with Phoenix? Tradition would be to dispose of a body through the airlock, not wanting to keep any extra mass on board; besides, most families assume that's what a space traveler would want, or they like the idea of their loved one still being out there in some way. But he didn't want to do that here. Somehow, he felt that he should return her to Jurassia, that that's what she would have wanted. And whether Magellan's great-great-whatever grandkids cared about their distant relative, or whether any of his descendants would still be there by the time her body got there, he felt confident that anyone in charge there would honor the request of Pirate Hunter Herne.

He found the passengers' suspension pods, but there were no empty ones he could use. He could wake a passenger and put her body in their place, but he wasn't ready to deal with that yet—the questions he'd have to answer, the complaints he'd have to listen to. He wandered around the ship looking for other options until he came to the area near where Phoenix had docked her ship. There he saw an unused suspension pod. She must have brought that over when she boarded the *Hispan-iola*, he thought. That would be perfect. He wheeled it back to the control room, opened it up, and carefully placed her body inside. He wished it could somehow bring her back, but he knew there was no technology that could do that now. The best he could hope for was preserving it for burial.

* * *

When he reached the Olympia space elevator, he was whisked away for a debriefing before he could even reach quarantine. He recognized Carol's face from the monitor on the elevator; the other six that were packed in the small room with him he didn't know.

"What happened!"

"Did you get it?"

"Where is she?"

"What about the two shuttles we saw launch?"

Herne just slouched back in his chair, overwhelmed, as their overlapping questions washed over him. When everyone else was finally silent for a moment, he opened his eyes, looked around, and sighed.

"Carol, stay. Everyone else, out!" and he pointed to the door. She had set him on this mission, and maybe he could handle this with one person, but he certainly couldn't with them all there.

The others sat in shock for a moment—none of them looked like they were used to taking orders this way—but one by one they stood up and walked out, eyeing Herne all the way, as if he might jump out of his chair and assault them. But he didn't have the energy to do that even if he wanted to.

When they had all left, Carol asked him gently, "Are you okay?"

"No, not really. But I did it."

"Tell me what you can. I'll take care of the rest later."

"I got it, it's still on the ship, but I'll take you to it. Phoenix is dead. She's ... I don't ... just make sure her body gets to Jurassia. Please." With that, he broke down in tears.

Carol's face took on a questioning look, but all she said was, "Okay. I will."

When Herne recovered, he stood up and said, "Let's go get it."

They walked back onto the ship, and Herne guided her to the cargo hold, taking the long away around the control room. "The passengers are still in suspension," he pointed out as they passed them, "and it looks like they're programmed to stay that way for months, so you can decide when you're ready to wake them up."

At the cargo hold, he pulled out the Eleusinian Totem and handed it to Carol. "Here you go. Get it back in place, please. I still want to do the Pilgrimage, see it properly."

"Or course. We'll get it out on a shuttle right away, and by the time you're ready to go there, it will be as if it had never left. I do have to ask you one thing, though: did you ever unwrap it?"

"Briefly, yes."

"Were there any ems active in the room when you did?"

Herne thought back. "Yes, I think I was talking to one. Methuselah, the one that helped me."

"Well, he probably earned it then. The hermetic case would stop it from affecting you or other biological systems, but unshielded it would likely be able to interact with a computational system. For a brief exposure, that probably just means cloning. Longer or more direct contact would have been very bad."

"I thought cloning ems was impossible, part of their quantum limitation? Even making multiple emulations of the same human brain has never worked, right?"

"Yes, with our known technology, yes, that's true. Somehow the aliens in the Totem can overcome that. They have a way to manipulate a system at the quantum level that allows a perfect copy without destroying the original. That's what makes it so dangerous. And I'm hoping that's all that happened. There's one way to find out: Methuselah?"

"Yes?"

"Yes? Wait, who was that?"

"There are two of you now," Carol explained. "Thank you —both—for your help in defeating Phoenix and restoring the Eleusinian Totem. You and Herne will be greatly rewarded for your heroic efforts."

Herne scoffed. "I don't need a reward. Just take care of Phoenix, and let me get on with the Pilgrimage and put this all behind me."

"Oh, I don't think you'll be able to put this behind you. You're a Pirate Hunter, like it or not."

"Well, I don't like it," Herne spat.

"That makes you the best kind."

* * *

Three weeks later, Herne was back at Eleusis, this time standing at the entrance to the labyrinth and surrounded by hundreds of other pilgrims. He wore a simple robe and sandals, as anonymous as he could be, given the circumstances. He had come from Olympia on a common shuttle, and nobody had a reason to pay close enough attention to notice that he was the only pilgrim that exited it. And so far, no one had recognized him since he landed; he had asked that his involvement be kept as quiet as possible—he didn't want to see himself on local news broadcasts—but he knew that wouldn't last forever. The news would eventually get out, not just on Olympia and in the local system, but throughout the galaxy, likely preceding him to whatever systems he might choose to visit in the future. But for now, at least, all he wanted was to get through the Pilgrimage in peace.

A cat brushed against his ankle, and he looked down. Big and orange, Herne tried to shoo it away—those were considered a sign of upcoming adventure, and Herne had had quite enough of that for a while—but it stuck by him until, finally, he bent over to pet it and offer it a small piece of salted meat. He kept walking toward the entrance and noticed the cat quietly following him. Just the one; other cats were doing their own thing, ignoring him and most of the other pilgrims, but apparently this one had taken a liking to him. Even as he passed into the labyrinth itself, the cat was there, so Herne decided it was time to place his first cup. "For Phoenix," he said, as he set it down on a ledge, filling it with water and a little honey. The cat jumped up on the ledge and started lapping it up as Herne walked on.

Herne wandered through the caves, choosing whichever paths seemed the least traveled, not that there was much distinction or any way to truly get lost in there. He set out cups for Magellan, as he had promised, for his parents, a relationship too far in the past to repair, even for his dinosaurs, knowing that he would likely never see them again. After two and a half days of walking and meditation, he reached the center, seeing again the Eleusinian Totem. It looked different in its natural environment, with dozens of other pilgrims standing in quiet contemplation. Herne wondered which of them might be affected by the lifeforms inside, and how. He kept back, not feeling a need to see it close up again. For him, the journey had been the important part, and as he set his past behind him along the way, he knew that his future could hold only one thing: more pirate hunting. He felt a nudge on his calf, looked down, and saw an orange cat again; it was too dim inside the caverns to tell if it was different or the same one that had followed him from the beginning. Either way, it pulled his attention away from the Totem; he turned and began his hike back to the entrance.

Chapter 31

Call me Castor. I've got mixed feelings about this. I know I'm supposedly the hero of Eleusis, but what do I know about running a warship? The *Umbriago* is nice, a lot different than an information courier like the *Hispaniola*. And I think I'll enjoy working with Herne. I respect him a lot for his bravery, and I hope I'm able to live up to his example (and, yes, my own example, as everyone likes to remind me) in the future. If we ever run into any more pirates, watch out! But I am a little jealous of my other self, being able to stay on the same ship, working with the same crew. This will be the biggest change for me since I became an em and joined the *Hispaniola* in the first place. But life is change, I guess, and since I somehow survived that adventure with my life, I suppose I shouldn't fear the change.

Herne is still down on Eleusis. After returning the Eleusinian Totem, he insisted on going through the whole Pilgrimage, as if none of this had happened. Even knowing what the Totem is, it was important to him, as part of his faith, to do it right, and I suspect he needs the time to process everything that happened. Once he's done, I think we move on. Phoenix's body is already on its way back to Jurassia, and I don't think he has any interest in returning there now. Maybe we follow Sybil, who no one has caught sight of yet; presumably, she's still in the system, but maybe she has found a way to sneak out already. I wouldn't put it past her, given the schemes she was able to come up with to help Phoenix. Maybe to Corsa—I know he feels bad about what happened to Phoenix and would like to punish the ones that made her what she was, especially knowing now that she was Magellan's niece. He's still legally a Pirate Hunter, after all, if he wants to make that the focus of his life now. Reluctant or not, I don't think he'll be able to avoid it completely.

And my twin? Yeah, that was a surprise when I realized I had been cloned by whatever process the aliens had. I don't expect to see him again, just like I never saw my human self after my original emulation. We'll go our separate ways, and if we do happen to run into each other again, we will have tra-versed very different timelines. It would be interesting to see how we both evolve, the similarities and differences we would see in each other after several centuries. The only pair of cloned ems in the galaxy. Perhaps we can arrange something after all.

Chapter 32

Call me Pollux. A new name for a new job. I'm now captain of the *Hispaniola*. I don't think I really deserve that honor, and it's going to be hard to live up to the standards of the previous captain, but someone needs to do it. I suppose I'll be remembered for how I led the em mutiny against Phoenix which is better than being remembered for surrendering to her in the first place, but I'll need to make sure the whole story is told. I won't pretend I'm something I'm not, and knowing what I knew about her plans with the Eleusinian Totem, anyone would have made the same decision.

We have a full crew again. Ani is taking over engineering for me, and we've replaced the many ems that were killed in the initial pirate attack or along the way. (Poor Takashi! If only he had survived to keep reminding me how right he had been all along.) The passengers were finally woken up and delivered to Olympia. Some were confused about how they were already through the Dyson sphere, wondering whether they could expect to be met at the elevator or if they'd have more difficulties with quarantine. I'm sure someone will tell them the story, more or less. But for me, I'm just happy they made it here, and I tell them they should feel the same.

We won't be long here, but I don't know where we're heading next. There are always messages to be delivered, and I'd be surprised if somewhere in our new info dump there's not a report on Phoenix, kudos for Herne, and a warning to watch out for Sybil, in case she manages to escape from the Olympia system. And, hopefully, exhortations to shut down the Corsan pirates that got Phoenix started on the path to piracy in the first place. If she hadn't been kidnapped, who knows what great things she might have done? So I feel bad for her demise, and I understand now why Herne was so upset by it, but as it was, it had to happen.

Whatever our future adventures, I'll keep up this journal, and I'll be wondering what is happening with my other half, so I hope he does the same. Then, even if we never meet up, we can send them along to each other and share our stories. And in sharing our stories maybe become a shared consciousness in a way, bigger than a single human or em. It will be interesting to see how that works out for us.

Acknowledgments

Thanks to Alex for suggestions on the nature of the pirates and the Totem. Thanks to Ben for insisting that there be cats; I hope he enjoys the dinosaurs, too. Thanks to Allison for more help and suggestions than I can even list, but most of all for encouraging me both to write this in the first place and to actually publish it. You are the best!

The ems were inspired by the work of Robin Hanson at George Mason University. I introduced limitations to meet the needs of the story, but his book, *The Age of Em,* provides a more realistic view of our possible em future. As for the other speculative technologies, I tried to keep them all within the bounds of physical possibility, though I admit that high-frequency gravitational wave communication is a bit of a stretch.

About the Author

Ron Stieger lives in Seattle with his wife and two sons. A hardware engineer by day, he is a graduate of Caltech and has designed satellite systems and coffee makers, and lots of things in between. He can't resist saying "Arrrr!!!" whenever someone talks about pirates. This is his first novel.